SPENSER

STARGAZER ALIEN MYSTERY BRIDES #3

TASHA BLACK

13TH STORY PRESS

Copyright © 2020 by 13th Story Press

All rights reserved. This book or any portion thereof may not be reproduced or used in any manner whatsoever without the express written permission of the publisher, except for the use of brief quotations in a book review.

13th Story Press

PO Box 506

Swarthmore, PA 19081

13thStoryPress@gmail.com

TASHA BLACK STARTER LIBRARY

Packed with steamy shifters, mischievous magic, billionaire superheroes, and plenty of HEAT, the Tasha Black Starter Library is the perfect way to dive into Tasha's unique brand of Romance with Bite!
Get your FREE books now at tashablack.com!

SPENSER

1

NATALIE

In her dream, Natalie was stretched out on a fluffy towel. The warmth of the sun kissed her cheeks as the sounds and scents of gently crashing waves permeated her senses.

A gentle breeze skittered pleasantly across her skin.

She didn't remember booking a trip to the beach, which was her first clue that she was dreaming, but now that she was there, it seemed like a great idea.

Suddenly, she was aware of a presence.

She looked up and saw a shadow spill across her body - a man's shadow, all wide shoulders and narrow hips.

She shaded her eyes with her hand and turned to look up at the person who was interrupting her relaxation.

Her breath caught in her throat.

It was him.

Spenser.

The hunky alien was bare-chested, his muscular form glistening in the sun.

"Natalie," he said, his deep voice playing on her senses.

She opened her mouth but couldn't speak.

Spenser lowered his big body to hers, caging her in those huge arms. He gazed into her eyes as her body burned for him.

She swore she could see universes colliding behind those dark eyes.

When he closed them, she closed hers too, every nerve ending in her body focused on her lips, awaiting his kiss.

He pressed his mouth to hers and she felt it to her toes, the need pouring off him hotter than the overhead sun, stoking her own desperate desire.

A seagull cried somewhere nearby, and then another.

She tried to focus on Spenser's mouth, and ignore the rhythmic calls.

But they only grew louder as the pressure of his body on hers began to fade away.

She tried to pull him closer, but he melted under her touch.

Natalie woke up at last, squinting into the early morning light with a handful of sheets, her alarm clock blaring beside her.

"Damn, Nat," she muttered to herself, reaching over to slap the alarm clock off. "You seriously need to get out more."

She staggered to the bathroom, suspecting that a hot shower, followed by a cup of coffee and some breakfast, would do a lot to ease her morning funk.

Filling her belly would be easy. Filling the emptiness left behind by her dream of romance might prove to be a little more difficult.

Natalie hadn't exactly been active on the dating scene lately. She had spent so much time focused on her career, that she wasn't sure she even remembered how to date.

"Who cares?" she muttered to herself. "Men are trouble anyway. You don't need one."

Which was true. She didn't need one.

But she kind of wanted one.

Maybe she should get a dog instead. She'd been thinking about it. They were big and slobbery, just like men. She wasn't sure how her landlord would feel about it, and having to pay a dog walker for when she was at work wasn't cheap. But maybe it was worth it if a little companionship from a loyal pet would keep her out of trouble.

Or maybe she didn't need *that* much help keeping her mind off men. After all, the man she was dreaming about wasn't even technically a man at all.

He was an alien. Which had its own baggage. But the real issue was that he was the brother of the alien mated to that dreadful Violet Locke, who was always interfering in police business and generally making a nuisance of herself. That whole group over on Crescent Street was trouble, and the last thing she needed was to be head-over-heels in helpless lust with one of them.

"Nope, nope, nope," she said to herself as she slipped under the steaming water.

But she suspected it might be too late for her.

She had talked with Spenser twice. Each time the air between them seemed to shimmer with the magnitude of their mutual lust.

She had walked away shaken both times, and hadn't been able to think of much else for a long time afterwards.

"Focus," she told herself. "Could be a big day today."

Chief Baker was about to announce the new Community First task force.

Natalie loved the work she did with the kids in the community, both on duty and off. She knew she was young to head up her own task force, but it felt like a great fit. And even if she didn't get chosen to lead, the mere existence of the Community First program in the first place would be the culmination of a lot of lobbying on her part.

"A big day, no matter what," she congratulated herself as she finished up her shower and headed back to her room to get dressed.

A few hours later, she was ensconced at her desk, a cup of coffee in one hand, and a phone in the other.

"What kind of cat is it?" she asked.

"I don't know, just... a black one," the lady on the other end said anxiously.

"A kitten? An older cat?" Natalie asked, jotting down notes.

"I guess kind of like a teenager," the woman replied, sniffing. "I just got him at the shelter last week."

"Like a young cat?" Natalie asked.

"Yes," the woman said.

"Is he wearing a collar?" Natalie asked.

"No, I want him to be able to chase mice," the woman said. "So I didn't put anything noisy on him."

Natalie managed to stifle her desire to give a lecture on why pets needed collars. The lady was clearly seeing the error of her ways.

"Is he micro-chipped?" she asked instead.

"Yes, he has a chip," the lady replied.

"That's great," Natalie praised her. "It was really smart for you to do that. And I'll bet when we find him, we can find a lightweight collar that won't slow him down when he's chasing mice, right?"

"Yes, officer, absolutely," the woman promised.

"Don't worry, we're going to do all we can to track him

down," Natalie told her. "And I will reconnect with you by the end of the day one way or the other."

"Th-thank you," the woman sniffed.

"That's my job," Natalie told her.

They hung up, and Natalie headed to the break room to refill her coffee. It was going to take time to call all the local shelters. If that didn't work out, she'd head over to Arbor Avenue and search on foot.

She thought bitterly about the time she'd wasted trying to find the last crop of lost pets, when it turned out her own mentor had rounded them up and taken them for training without telling anyone.

Harvey Smalls was a good mayor, whose heart was absolutely in the right place. And he was usually a great mentor, especially since Natalie didn't have much support from her family. She had no siblings, and she wasn't close with her parents, so she appreciated the guidance she got from Harvey all the more. And he was usually right on the money with his advice, both career and personal.

But she had to admit that his recent efforts to single-handedly make Stargazer into some kind of model town had been a bit misguided, at best.

And Natalie wondered if fewer skateboarders and barking dogs would really make any impression at all on the big corporation that was coming to Stargazer to look at opening an executive campus in town.

She shook her head as she poured out another cup of joe.

"Busy morning?" Lance, one of the other officers asked.

She wasn't really what you would call close with any of her coworkers, but Lance was probably the one she would be most likely to call a friend. He was kind, and seemed to like the job almost as much as she did.

"Lost cat at 108 Arbor Avenue," she told him.

"What color?" he asked.

"Black," she replied. "Young cat, male."

"Hey," Lance said. "Do you think that could have anything to do with the black cat those people found at 110 Arbor Avenue?"

"Do I think the lost cat at 108 has anything to do with a found cat at 110?" Natalie asked, laughing. "Yeah, I'm pretty sure it does. What's the name of the homeowner at 110 again?"

"Lemme check," Lance said.

She followed him to his desk.

"It's Nuñez," he told her, reading his notes. "I'll call them."

"Nah, it's my lunch break anyway," Natalie said. "I'll stop by on my way to Burger Planet."

"Suit yourself," Lance said.

A few minutes later, she drove down Arbor Avenue and parked in the shade of a scarlet-leafed tree. When she stepped up onto the porch of 110, she could hear the happy sounds of children squealing over something, presumably the neighbor's cat.

She rang the bell.

A man opened the door, he was carrying a half of a peanut butter sandwich. A small toddler in a rainbow dress clung to his leg and looked up at Natalie with wide eyes.

In the background someone was chanting, "*Cat! Cat! Cat!*"

"Are you here about the cat?" the father asked hopefully.

"I'm here about the cat," she confirmed.

"Thank God," he said.

The chanting child appeared with the other half of the

peanut butter sandwich. She looked nearly identical to her sister. This poor guy had more than he could handle.

A small cat trailed in the child's wake, appearing to be more interested in the sandwich in her hand than in the girl.

"Who does it belong to?" he asked.

"Would you believe me if I told you it belongs to the lady next door?" she asked.

He threw his head back and laughed.

"She just got it last week," Natalie said, smiling. "Do you want me to bring it over?"

"No, no, the girls and I will bring the cat back to its owner, right girls?" he asked hopefully.

The girls took the news with good cheer, but in fairness, they probably didn't know what he was talking about.

Natalie headed back out to her car and watched as the dad carried the cat over to the house next door, toddlers in tow, and presented the missing feline to its very grateful owner.

He waved to Natalie on his way back home with the kids.

"Thank you so much, Officer West," the cat's owner called to her tearfully.

"My pleasure," Natalie called to them. "You all have a great day."

Moments like these were the best part of the job. Unlike some of her colleagues, Natalie hadn't gotten into this line of work for over-the-top excitement of any kind. She loved her town and wanted to help.

She hopped back in the car and had almost made it to Burger Planet when her radio crackled to life.

"Hey Merle," she said.

"They need you over at the mayor's house," Merle said

in a worried voice, abandoning any attempt at police jargon and just sounding like a person in distress.

"What's up?" Natalie asked.

"Just get there as soon as you can," Merle said, clicking off.

2
NATALIE

Natalie stood in the mayor's study, a pleasant, shadowy room where she had spent countless quiet hours talking with her mentor about her dreams for the community.

Today, the brocade drapes had been thrown open to let in muted sunlight from the shaded patio on the other side of French doors.

It would have been pretty, except that the prone, lifeless body of Harvey Smalls lay on the floor behind his desk.

Natalie wrapped her arms around her shoulders and willed herself to breathe.

"This looks open and shut to me," Chief Baker said. "He had a known allergy. There's an open container of food on the desk. Looks like he just didn't have his EpiPen handy."

"He always had it handy," Natalie said automatically.

"Well, maybe not handy enough," the chief replied.

"Check the top desk drawer," Natalie said, turning to look out the French doors and into the mayor's idyllic backyard to try and center herself.

She could hear someone rummaging around in the desk behind her.

"Nothing in here, Chief," Lance said.

"That can't be right," Natalie said. "He always kept one near him, always. He was incredibly careful about his allergy."

She stepped over and looked in the drawer herself.

Lance was right. There were sticky notes, pens and pencils, and a few papers. But there was no EpiPen.

She sighed.

In the next room, she could hear a low, animal whine.

"Barker Posey," she said, remembering the mayor's beloved dog.

"We put her in her crate," Lance said. "She was kind of freaking out."

Of course she was. The poor thing was probably confused and terrified. Natalie was feeling a bit of both herself.

"I'll take her home with me," Natalie said. "Is that okay, Chief?"

"Sure," Chief Baker replied. "It's that or the shelter. He doesn't have any family nearby that I know of."

"Look, I'm going to deal with the dog for now," Natalie said. "But please, promise me we'll keep this case open. Harvey would never have eaten a bite of something without checking for nuts. And he definitely wouldn't have been without an EpiPen. And the food right on the table, that feels too convenient to me. There's something fishy about all of this."

"Natalie," the chief said. "Walk with me."

She allowed him to take her arm and walk her down the hall to where the mayor's dog shivered in her crate.

The enormous Saint Bernard looked almost small with

fear. She gazed up at Natalie, her dark eyes filled with sadness.

I hear you, girl.

"Listen, I know how much the mayor meant to you," the chief said kindly. "No one would blame you for having big feelings on this. But it's clearly a terrible, tragic accident."

"But Chief—" Natalie began.

"I'm going to have to ask you to let this go," Chief Baker said. "We're not going to investigate this as a force, and I'm asking you not to investigate it on your own. You're not thinking clearly right now, but I know you care about this community. You wouldn't want to upset everyone over something that's clearly not a murder."

When he used the word *murder* it gave her a moment of pause. She had been thinking there was a little more to it. But would someone really *murder* the mayor?

"I want you to take the rest of the week off, with pay," the chief went on. "Take some time and mourn. We'll be here when you get back."

"Thank you," she heard herself say. Her voice sounded far away.

"This force is a family," he said, thumping her once on the back. "Call if you need anything. Try to get some rest, and remember to eat. Margaret will stop by with a casserole."

Margaret was Chief Baker's wife. She was famous for her numerous, inedible casseroles. And for her warm hugs.

"Thank you," Natalie said again, grabbing Barker Posey's leash. "I'll just get her out of here."

3

SPENSER

Spenser strolled down the street, past the shops of Stargazer, watching the colorful leaves drift onto the sidewalk ahead of him.

Halloween decorations festooned the store windows. Spenser eyed them with suspicion.

From all he could glean of human behavior, humans did not wish to be frightened. They went to great lengths to avoid scary surprises, especially when it came to their children. Spenser had tried, but could not fully piece together the reasoning behind the many ratings for movies.

His friend, Dr. Bhimani, had explained that the ratings were aimed to warn people about what things in the movie might frighten children, without ruining the story.

Now suddenly the whole town seemed to be celebrating this strange holiday. Monsters, witches, and ample gore were on public display.

And somehow the whole thing was designed for children.

He spotted a mannequin in a store window that was holding its own severed head, along with a sign that warned patrons they might lose their own heads when they observed the shop's low prices. Apparently, there were distinctions between what was considered fun-scary, and what was just plain scary, that were lost on Spenser.

He finally reached his destination and stood outside for a moment, feeling restless.

His brothers Hannibal and Fletcher both had mates now, filling their lives with love and pleasure.

Only Spenser remained alone.

It was no surprise to him. While his brothers had adapted easily to this new world, Spenser still struggled to understand humans.

His mate would help him, when he found her. For now, it was still difficult.

His brothers had suggested that he go someplace where people shared his interests. They explained that he might be more likely to find his mate in such a location, and that even if he didn't, he might make some friends.

The glass storefront he faced had a sign in the window.

The Silver Club - Fun Activities for Adults - Every Day of the Week - All Are Welcome

Spenser was an adult and he liked fun activities. Besides, he had come to understand that the word *adult* was often a satellite word to mating activities.

How he longed to find a woman to call his mate.

He was here today because they were hosting something called a *Puzzler's Brunch*. And Spenser's favorite human activity was solving puzzles and crosswords. If this place wasn't the key to finding a mate, he had no idea what was.

But somehow, now that he was here, it was hard to go inside.

A pair of young women walked past, eating ice cream cones.

He nodded to them, and they both giggled, their eyes running hungrily all over his body. He felt a shallow frisson of desire, but not the inexorable pull he knew a mate's gaze would bring.

Frustrated, he pushed open the door of *The Silver Club*.

"Well, hello there," a lady said, her voice rough and raspy.

He looked down to see that she had dark brown eyes and a head of fluffy white hair.

"Hello," he replied, noticing with disappointment that she was also not his mate.

"My name is Darlene. Are you looking for someone?" the woman asked.

"No," Spenser said. "I am Spenser and I am looking for the Puzzler's Brunch."

"Well, this is it," Darlene said, spreading her arms wide.

A large table at the center of the room was set up with jigsaw puzzles. Four other people, all with white hair, sat at the table, chatting, eating fruit and danishes and putting together the pieces to form cohesive images.

He'd been hoping for word or logic puzzles, but jigsaw puzzles were fun as well.

"Come on in," Darlene said. "Everyone, this is Spenser."

"Marge," one of the women said, tapping her own chest. "My, aren't you a tall one. You can't reach the puzzle on the top shelf, can you?'

Everyone turned, as if in great suspense.

Spenser walked to the big bookshelf that lined the far wall. Sure enough, a lone puzzle box sat on the top shelf.

He lifted it down and handed it to Marge, after blowing some dust off the top.

"Ohhh," Marge said, looking as pleased as if he had handed her a briefcase full of intergalactic credits.

The others gave him a small burst of applause.

"Wonderful," another lady whispered to Darlene, who had seated herself at the table.

He had only retrieved a puzzle, but their response was gratifying.

Spenser smiled benevolently down at the group.

"Sit down, son," a man with wrinkled brown skin and an impressive beard told him, indicating the chair next to him. "I'm Al."

"It is a pleasure to meet you," Spenser told him.

"What brings you to the Silver Club?" Al asked.

"I am new to Stargazer," Spenser said, carefully not saying he was an alien. Lots of people were mistrustful of aliens on this planet, though they loved making movies about them. "My brothers thought I might make new friends if I visited a place where other people had the same interests."

"What are your interests?" Darlene asked.

"Puzzles and crosswords," Spenser said. "I like solving things."

For a moment he felt a little silly not being interested in something more important.

"Well, you came to the right place," Al laughed, and slapped him on the leg.

They puzzled on quietly for a little while. Spenser wasn't sure what the picture was meant to be, but most of the pieces were red and white.

Darlene and Al seemed to be fond of looking for edges, which left Marge and Spenser to do the middle parts.

That suited Spenser fine, he preferred a challenge.

Down at the other side of the table, two more guests were working on a different puzzle.

"Why can't I find this one?" Marge complained after a few minutes. "It should be white with a red stripe."

"May I see?" Spenser asked.

She pushed a collection of pieces his way sadly. The middle piece would connect them all if they could find it.

He studied the shapes.

Marge was right, the missing piece should be white with a red stripe, but there appeared to be a shadow moving across the image.

He scanned the spread-out pieces on the table, sliding his hand through them, looking for something specific.

"Here," he said triumphantly, handing her a piece.

"But this is gray and red," she said.

"Just give it a try," he told her.

Her face lit up as it clicked into place.

"How did you know?" she asked.

"It was the shadow making the white part look gray," he told her. "Not everything is exactly what it seems."

Al clapped for him again.

"That's a life lesson too," Darlene agreed.

"You have such good eyes," Marge decided, beaming at him. "You remind me of my grandson."

She painstakingly removed a tablet device from her oversized purse and swiped through photos until she got to the right one. "There he is."

Spenser gazed down at the picture. In it, Marge was smiling up at a young man who had an arm around her.

Spenser could see no resemblance between himself and the boy whatsoever. But he sensed it would be impolite to mention it.

"That's a very nice picture," he told her instead. "You two look very happy."

"Thank you," she told him, putting her tablet away. "He lives far away, but I do love seeing him."

Darlene winked at Spenser from across the table as Marge fussed with her bag, as if approving of what he had said.

His brothers had been right. He *had* made friends.

But he was no closer to finding a mate.

4

NATALIE

Natalie wandered the streets of Stargazer, Barker Posey's leash slack in her hand, trying her best to process what had just happened.

The big dog wasn't capering or pulling. She walked along slowly, looking about as lost as Natalie felt.

Who was Natalie without her mentor?

She had already begun asking that after his misguided efforts to better the town had gotten him into hot water. But now he was dead. There was no working through that.

And who was she without her job?

She'd just been dismissed from doing the only thing she really wanted to do at a time like this - work. And she was banned from investigating the case, if there even was one.

Apparently, she was now just someone who wandered the streets aimlessly with a very large dog.

Her phone buzzed, startling her temporarily back into her surroundings. She ignored the phone, but looked up at the building in front of her. The glossy, painted door had brass numbers hanging from it.

221B

"Seriously," Natalie said to herself.

She might have thought she was wandering aimlessly, but her feet had brought her straight to Crescent Street - straight to Violet Locke.

And also to Violet's friend, Jana Watson, and the three aliens who had somehow helped Vi solve the case involving the mayor's attempted good deeds.

Much as she did not want to ask Vi for help investigating the mayor's death, Natalie had been told in no uncertain terms that the department wouldn't look into it.

So the options were to work with Vi, or to work by herself. She supposed her feet had carried her here for a reason.

It still wasn't an easy decision.

If only Vi had just an ounce of humility, it might be different. But she had all but rubbed her victories in the police department's face each time she solved a local mystery before the department could.

And there was an even bigger reason to stay away. A big, muscular reason, with a smile that made her feel like…

"…melting," a familiar deep voice intoned.

She turned to see Spenser headed her way. And there was that smile. She felt her cheeks flush.

"What?" was all she could manage.

"Hello, Officer West," the big man said. "I was just saying that I was glad to see you, because my ice cream is melting."

Sure enough, he was carrying a gigantic, melting dish of ice cream in each hand.

"Wow," she said. "Hi."

"I couldn't decide between sundaes, so I bought both," he explained. "Now I need help eating them, and opening the door."

He wasn't wrong. There was no way he could get inside on his own with all that ice cream.

She took an instant to consider, but it was impossible to say no.

Good looking man, good looking ice cream, and she certainly had no place else to go.

"Is it okay for me to bring the dog inside?" she asked hopefully.

"Of course," he said. "But I think we should eat these on the patio. They seem very messy."

"That sounds nice," Natalie replied, realizing that it did.

"My key is in my pocket," he told her, glancing down at his front right pocket.

"Oh, uh, okay," she replied, eyeing him guardedly.

She could barely look at him without wanting to climb him like a tree. Did she really want to stick her hand in his pocket?

Yes. Yes, she did.

But she probably shouldn't.

She contemplated what a bad idea it was as she approached him and reached out her hand.

Up close like this, she could smell him, spicy and warm over the sweet, fruity scent of the ice cream. And she found herself wanting nothing more than to lick that melted ice cream off his hands until he begged for more.

Instead, she slid her hand into his pocket as quickly as she could and tried to ignore the hard muscle of his thigh long enough to snag the key and pull it out.

Her cheeks were practically on fire as she unlocked the door. She could sense his presence behind her, and feel the lust pouring off him as if they had been interrupted in the middle of lovemaking instead of just opening a door.

The hallway was dim. As Natalie's eyes adjusted, her other senses amped up.

She could smell the tang of the cherries on top of Spenser's sundaes. Barker Posey was panting loudly, and she was momentarily glad for the big dog's presence. Between the dog and the ice cream, it was very unlikely that they would somehow start making out before they reached the back door. She could already see the light pouring out of the transom. They just had to make it a few more steps.

Sunlight burst in, nearly blinding her.

"Officer West," Jana Watson blurted out, her bright voice filled with surprise.

"I'm not here on official business," Natalie said right away.

"Oh," Jana replied. "That's good..."

Natalie could hear the unsaid *Then why are you here?* even though Jana was far too polite to voice it.

"Here, I've got the door," Jana said. "Guys, Officer West is here."

Natalie wondered what they'd been doing outside.

A ridiculous image of them all trying to pull the thumbtacks out of a crime map and hide it away before she made it out came into her mind. She had to close her eyes to shake it.

She felt almost guilty looking out at the patio and seeing Violet and Hannibal chatting over a glass of iced tea while Fletcher pulled weeds from the tiny lawn.

"Hi," she said, with an awkward wave.

"Officer West," Vi said. "This is a surprise."

"I'm not here on official business," Natalie assured everyone again. "And you can call me Natalie."

"Natalie," Vi said thoughtfully, trying it out.

"I found her standing outside with her magnificent dog," Spenser offered.

"That's not her dog," Vi said, before Natalie could correct him. "That's the mayor's dog, Barker Posey."

"You're right," Natalie said, hating herself for being impressed. After all, how many Saint Bernards were running around Stargazer?

"Something's happened to the mayor," Vi said.

It wasn't a question.

"Yes," Natalie said, trying to think of the right words to explain it, but coming up short.

Suddenly, she was completely exhausted. It was too hard to decide where to begin, how to tell them what happened and why she was suspicious.

Her head felt like it was made of lead.

"Why don't you sit down?" Jana suggested, indicating a spot at the picnic table.

Spenser sat beside her, and she felt oddly sheltered by his big body.

He pushed both sundaes toward her.

She chose the hot fudge and he pulled the marshmallow back with a smile, as if he'd gotten the one he wanted. Or he was just happy that she had.

She toyed with the whipped cream with her spoon, suddenly feeling like she might never eat again.

"Take a bite," Jana suggested, sitting down across from her. "You'll feel better. When was the last time you ate?"

It had been morning.

She dipped her spoon deeper and took a bite instead of answering. The flavors exploded in her mouth, the cold ice cream invigorating her even as the hot fudge warmed her. Maybe she wasn't going on a hunger strike after all. Still, resisting ice cream for almost ten seconds had to be a personal record.

"Oh, wow, that's so good," she said, closing her eyes.

"Why don't we let Barker Posey off the leash?" Vi suggested. "She looks like she could use a nap."

Natalie handed over the leash and Vi unsnapped it.

Barker Posey trotted around the yard, sniffing things.

"She smells our landlord's dog," Vi said.

"She's going to find Maybelle's water bowl in a minute," Jana said, smiling.

Sure enough, Barker Posey bounded back onto the patio a moment later and Natalie could hear her slurping water, though she couldn't see past Spenser to get eyes on the dog.

"Keep eating," Spenser advised, as though she had looked in his direction for a clue about what to do next.

She took another bite anyway, not because he had told her to, but because it was good.

The others gave her space. There was no sound except the birds calling to each other in the little garden and Barker Posey's rhythmic slurps.

"The mayor is dead," Natalie heard herself say around a bite of banana.

"Oh," Jana said sadly.

Spenser patted Natalie's back with a giant hand.

Vi nodded to herself as if this was exactly as she had suspected.

Natalie resisted the urge to slap her. Barely.

Fletcher came over and sat beside Jana.

"Chief Baker thinks it was an accident," Natalie said. "There's an open box of treats on his desk, and it's pretty clear that he died of an allergic reaction."

"Anaphylaxis?" Vi said, shaking her head. "That doesn't make sense. He was never without an EpiPen."

"Right," Natalie said, begrudgingly impressed. "How did you know that?"

"The leather pen case," Vi replied. "It was a little too big, and he carried it in his right breast pocket."

"True," Natalie admitted.

"How did that tell you it was an EpiPen?" Jana asked, looking back and forth between them.

"Because he was right-handed," Natalie said. "He would have kept a pen in his left breast pocket to grab for writing. Anything in his right pocket would be something he wanted to have close, but didn't think he'd actually use."

Vi gave her a reluctant half smile.

"Anyway," Natalie said, "there was no EpiPen anywhere at the scene. Not on his person, or even in the desk. It's totally out of character for him, especially when eating homemade treats. He knew the risks."

"The treats on his desk were homemade?" Vi asked.

"It looked that way," Natalie replied.

"Who made them?" Vi asked.

Shit.

"I-I wasn't paying close enough attention," Natalie admitted.

"Why not?" Vi asked.

"Vi, her friend just died," Jana reminded Vi quietly.

"Yeah, right," Vi said. "Sorry about that."

"No, you were right," Natalie said. "I should have been paying attention to that. I should have been paying attention to everything."

"So what were you paying attention to?" Vi asked.

Jana rolled her eyes as if her friend were a lost cause.

But it was actually a good question. What had she noticed?

"The drapes were thrown open," Natalie said slowly.

"They're never open. Most likely it was done by one of the first responders on the scene, to make it easier for the guys to look around, but not necessarily."

She automatically reached for her notepad, but of course she wasn't in uniform.

"I'm on it," Vi told her, whipping out a notepad of her own.

"And I could hear Barker Posey whimpering in her crate in the other room," she went on.

"Did the police put her in the crate when they arrived?" Vi asked.

"That's what they told me," Natalie replied.

"Did you notice anything else?" Vi asked.

Natalie shook her head.

"The chief got me out of there pretty fast. I think he was worried about me. We're all pretty close down at the station. Anyway, he let me take the dog and he gave me the rest of the week off with pay, and then he walked me out."

"Do you trust him?" Vi asked.

"Of course," Natalie said, offended.

"Then why are you here?" Vi asked.

"He's not going to investigate," Natalie said.

"How do you know?" Vi asked.

"He told me he isn't," Natalie said. "He asked me to stay out of it too."

"Why?" Vi asked.

"He said it was for the good of the town," Natalie said bitterly. "He said that digging into something that's obviously a tragic accident will only upset people."

"Hmm," Vi said.

"I care about this town," Natalie told them. "I really do."

"We know that," Jana told her.

"But something about this doesn't feel right to me," Natalie said.

Spenser wrapped an arm around her, and Jana patted her hand like a mother comforting a small child.

But it was Vi's scowl of annoyed concentration that made her feel better. Her wheels were turning, and that meant that Natalie had been right to be suspicious.

"I'll take the case," Vi said, giving a single, firm nod and then getting up from the table.

5
NATALIE

Natalie held her phone to her ear as she exited the vehicle with Vi and her friends. On the other end, Lila from the station was gabbing on and on about office gossip.

"...*Anyway,*" Lila said at last, "I'll check out that traffic cam on the mayor's street for you and get back to you shortly."

"Thank you so much," Natalie said, meaning it. "And please *don't* tell anyone."

Natalie had covered for Lila a few times. Hopefully, that would keep her quiet. The last thing Natalie needed was to get on the chief's bad side.

Vi slammed the driver's side door of the old ice cream truck she now used as a crime-solving vehicle, and joined everyone else on the sidewalk.

"Can't you leave the dog in the car?" Vi asked Natalie.

"It gets hot in there fast," Natalie said, clutching Barker Posey's leash protectively. "Plus, she's my alibi if anyone sees me there."

"You mean sees *us* there," Vi corrected her.

Natalie sighed.

She knew Vi needed to see the crime scene for herself - it was a condition of her taking the case. And it was a good idea. Vi was very observant. Natalie knew that much.

But she was also risking her career by sneaking a private investigator into the mayor's home.

The dead mayor's home.

On the other hand, what else was she supposed to do?

"Come on," she said quickly, before she had a chance to change her mind.

The group strode onward, toward the block where the mayor's little blue house was shaded by two magnolias.

"We'll go in the back," Natalie suggested. "Through the alleyway."

Barker Posey's ears lifted slightly. She knew she was nearly home, and Natalie was afraid she thought the mayor might be there.

"We're only going for a minute," she whispered to the hopeful dog. "He's not there."

Spenser moved closer to walk beside her.

"It will be painful for you to go to your friend's house because he is dead," he pointed out kindly in his deep voice.

He was an alien and had maybe missed the finer points of how to be sympathetic, but his heart was definitely in the right place.

"Yes," she said. "That's true."

"I will be with you," he told her.

"Oh, no, it's bad enough that Vi needs to come in," she said. "The rest of you will have to stay outside."

He didn't reply.

He was silent, but his mouth had formed a thin line of displeasure.

"It's just a house," Natalie said. "Sure, he was the mayor, but it wasn't anything fancy."

"I have no desire to see this house," Spenser said firmly.

"Oh," she replied. "You just looked kind of ticked off."

"What does it mean to be *ticked off*?" he asked. "I have no bugs on me, if this is what you mean."

"No," she said, smiling. "It means annoyed or a little bit angry."

"Ah," he said. "Yes. I am ticked off."

"Why?" she asked. "I might get in trouble, but your friend Vi won't be in danger. I will protect her."

"But who will protect you?" he asked.

She looked up at him in surprise.

His dark eyes looked especially soulful. His expression wasn't annoyed, it was pained.

"I can protect myself," she said slowly, feeling a little ticked off herself. "I'm a trained police officer. I aced my hand-to-hand training at the academy. But I don't think it's going to come up."

He turned away, as if he were trying to focus on the trees and the houses instead of talking with her.

"Is there something else?" she asked.

"Yes," he said. "But we will talk of it later."

She nodded.

It was impossible not to think about their attraction, and the deal with the men from Aerie.

In the papers it said they were here to search for their bonded mates, and that once they found them, they were extremely protective.

She was certainly attracted to him, but it felt unlikely that she was his mate. They had only met by happenstance. And he had said nothing about it.

The interviews with the Stargazer Three always began

with the women talking about how the one called Bond had wooed Posey immediately, just moments after they met.

Those first three women to meet aliens had to learn everything about the men from Aerie in a hurry.

Now the world knew more. And none of it led Natalie to think it was likely that she was Spenser's mate. She was sure they would be interested in women who were more adventurous and outgoing. And they probably expected stuff like…

"Going in the back door?" Vi asked, coming up to join them.

"What?" Natalie coughed.

"Are we going in the back door?" Vi repeated. "To stay less visible?"

"Yeah," Natalie said, glad for the distraction.

"We should have everyone else spread out," Vi suggested. "They can signal us if anyone is coming."

"Good thinking," Natalie said. "I'm going to head in with Barker Posey by myself now. That way if anyone is already there, I've got good reason to be inside. I'll signal to you if the coast is clear."

Vi nodded and headed back to the rest of the group.

"Be careful," Spenser intoned. "Please."

"I will," Natalie said without looking at him.

She was afraid if she looked in his eyes, he might read her thoughts, and she would be infinitely embarrassed if he knew she was thinking about being his mate.

She headed to the back gate and lifted the clasp.

Barker Posey headed right to her favorite tree and squatted to pee. Natalie waited for her, taking the opportunity to glance around and be sure no one was watching her.

Though it was a beautiful day, none of the neighbors

were out on their decks. When Barker was finished, they jogged up onto the back porch.

The mayor's back door was locked, which was a first. But the key was thoughtfully left under a potted plant next to the door.

She slipped it in, turned the knob, and they were in.

The house felt quieter than usual. The mayor's classical music wasn't playing, and he wasn't on the phone chatting up one person or another, trying to cajole the whole town into bettering itself.

Barker Posey sat politely, looking up at the cookie jar on the kitchen counter that held her treats.

Natalie took a moment to pull one out for her.

"Hello," she called out, as the dog made quick work of the biscuit.

Natalie headed out into the living room and then crossed over into the dining room, finally peeking her head into the study.

The downstairs was clear. So far, so good.

She trotted up the steps, Barker Posey at her heels.

After finding the bedrooms and bath empty, she headed back down to the kitchen and waved at the window.

Vi waved back from the alley and then headed up the rear steps, holding something.

"Is that a magazine?" Natalie asked as Vi came in.

"It's my cover," Vi said. "If anyone asks why I'm here, it was delivered to the wrong house."

"Nice," Natalie said as she led the way to the study.

She had a hard time even looking at the room, though she knew it was her duty to help Vi search it.

"What are you doing?" Vi asked her. "Go get the dog's stuff. Let me concentrate."

Natalie knew she should argue, but she felt nothing but sweet relief as she headed out to the living room.

She grabbed a reusable shopping bag from the table by the front door and took it over to the dog's toy bin.

Barker Posey followed with interest.

Natalie had nearly filled the bag when she heard a loud whistle outside.

She froze, realizing they were being warned.

"Vi," she called out softly.

"Almost done," Vi called back. "Buy me some time."

But the front door was already opening.

"Hello," Natalie called, so as not to startle whoever was entering.

She was relieved to see it was one of her nicer colleagues, Lance. He wasn't likely to make trouble for them.

"Natalie, what are you doing here?" Lance asked, looking a little scandalized.

"I had to get Barker Posey's stuff," Natalie said, allowing herself to look at little guilty. "Please don't tell the chief I was here. I was so upset when I left before that I didn't even think to get her toys or her food."

"Oh," Lance said, looking a little relieved. "Sure, go ahead and get her stuff. But then you better get out of here, the chief is on his way."

"What for?" Natalie asked. "I thought he didn't want to investigate."

"He just wanted to make sure we cleaned up after ourselves today," Lance said. "And get the place locked down until the estate attorney gets in touch. As a courtesy to the mayor's memory."

"That's nice," Natalie allowed.

"I guess," Lance said. "Are you sure you're okay?"

His back was to the study, so he didn't see Vi poke her face out and give Natalie a thumbs up.

Natalie automatically smiled back at her.

Lance got a funny look on his face.

Crap.

He was asking if she was okay after the death of her mentor, and she was grinning at him.

Way to act normal.

"It's so kind of you to ask," Natalie said, trying to give a reason for the smile. "It's really good to have a close colleague like you."

"Er, thanks," Lance said.

She wasn't really lying. It was nice, and they had always been friendly, if not particularly close.

She hoped she wasn't giving him the wrong idea.

Meanwhile, Vi looked desperate.

She couldn't go out the French doors of the study without making too much noise. And she certainly couldn't walk out into the living room where Lance and Natalie were.

If Natalie stopped talking with Lance for even a moment, he would surely head right into the study and find Vi.

If only they had one more person, they could create a diversion. Natalie glanced over at Barker Posey and had a sudden thought.

The mayor was very proud of his dog's training. He had shown it off to Natalie a million times.

Barker Posey responded to hand controls as well as to vocal commands. The mayor felt there was no excuse for not training a canine. Their intelligence made training essential in his eyes - the smarter the dog, the more training it needed.

And Barker Posey was super smart.

Natalie coughed to get the dog's attention.

As soon as she looked up, Natalie gave her the signal for *play dead.*

Barker Posey did her late owner credit, flopping suddenly to the ground, bouncing stiffly a little, for effect.

"Oh, my God," Natalie cried, feigning despair.

"What happened to her?" Lance asked.

"She has seizures," Natalie wailed, kneeling at the dog's side, knowing Barker Posey would not get up until she heard her release word. "She needs her medication."

"Where is it?" Lance asked.

"Upstairs, in the bathroom, I think," Natalie cried.

Lance dashed up the stairs, two at a time.

"Check the medicine cabinet," Natalie yelled.

Vi shot out of the study and dashed past Natalie and the still-playing-dead Barker Posey and headed for the kitchen door, where she waited.

Natalie shooed her on.

Vi pointed upward.

Oh. Of course.

If Lance looked out the bathroom window, he would see her making her escape across the backyard.

"Okay, Barker Posey, good girl," Natalie said quietly.

The dog hopped up and shook herself vigorously.

"Never mind, Lance, she's okay," Natalie called up.

"Are you sure?" he yelled down.

"Very sure," she said. "She's fine now."

As soon as his feet hit the steps, Vi headed out the back door.

"Wow, you're right, look at her," Lance said, gazing at Barker Posey in disbelief.

"I guess I'll swing her by the vet to be sure," Natalie said weakly.

"Good idea," Lance said. "That was really weird. You really should get out of here though - the chief will be here any minute."

"Roger that," Natalie said.

She had barely gotten the leash back on the dog when there was a commotion in the backyard. There was some kind of shouted exchange that she couldn't quite make out, and then the door swung open.

"What the hell is going on here?" Chief Baker bellowed, striding in the back door, leading Vi by the arm.

6

NATALIE

Natalie fought the urge to scream with frustration.

"And what are *you* doing here?" the chief demanded, glaring at her.

"She just came back for the dog's stuff," Lance said automatically.

"I forgot her food," Natalie said.

"And her medication," Lance added.

The chief looked like he was going to explode. The vein in his temple was doing that thing it did when he was about to lose his cool.

"You two don't have anything to do with *this* person being here, do you?" he asked, glancing at Vi.

"I told you, I'm only here to return the paper," Vi said, waving the magazine weakly in her free hand. "I got it by mistake."

"Let me see that," the chief said, snatching it from her and reading the mailing label out loud. "Harvey Smalls."

He sighed through his nose, clearly frustrated, and let go of Vi.

"Get out of here," he told Vi. "And you..."

He turned to Natalie and frowned for a long moment.

"I hate to do this," he said at last. "I asked you to stay away and you didn't. You should have called if you needed something for the dog. I would have gotten it for you, and you know it."

"But, Chief—" Natalie began.

"—No, no, no," he said. "Don't piss on me and tell me it's raining. I asked you not to investigate, and a few hours later I find you here with a private detective and a paper-thin cover story. I don't have to be a genius to connect the dots."

Natalie opened her mouth and closed it again.

"I hate to do it," the chief continued. "But you're suspended for two weeks. If I catch you here again, or anywhere near this non-case, I'll fire you. Do I make myself clear?"

"Yes, sir," Natalie replied.

"Okay, then, get out of here," he said.

Natalie headed out the back door right behind Vi. Even Barker Posey walked slowly, as if chastened.

"I'm sorry we got caught," Vi said as they crossed the yard.

"It's okay," Natalie said. "I don't know why it didn't occur to me the chief would come in the back door."

"Hm," Vi said.

"Hey, how did you do that anyway?" Natalie said.

"Do what?" Vi asked.

"Get his name onto the magazine," Natalie said.

"It was in the alleyway when we got here," Vi laughed.

"So it was really his?" Natalie asked.

"Yup," Vi said.

"Fantastic," Natalie said.

And even though it had been probably the worst day of her life, she laughed.

"Well, I guess we're headed back to 221B," Vi said.

"Actually, I should probably go home and talk to my landlord about the dog," Natalie told her. "If it's okay I'll swing by later."

"Of course," Vi said. "We'll drop you off at your place."

"Thanks," Natalie said.

Ten minutes later, Natalie and Barker Posey walked up to her own apartment.

It was a U-shaped building designed around a pretty little garden. Natalie's apartment was in the center, looking out over the fountain that was the showpiece of the garden.

Instead of going inside to her unit, she rang her landlord's bell. After a few minutes, the door swung open.

Mr. Lancaster looked a lot like Mark Twain, if Mark Twain had just taken a large swallow of spoiled milk.

"No, no, no, no, no," he said before he was even finished opening the door.

"But I haven't—" Natalie began.

"You don't have to say anything," Mr. Lancaster blurted. "That dog does not set one paw onto my property and that's the end of it."

"My mentor died and there's no one else to take her," Natalie said.

"Oh, I'm sure there's someone else," Mr. Lancaster said, glancing at his watch. "The pound is open until six."

"I'm *not* taking her to the pound," Natalie said.

"Well, you're not coming in here," he replied firmly. "It's in your lease."

She took a deep breath and let it out slowly. He was right. But she had been hoping he would make an exception.

"Look," she said. "I'll find someplace else to stay with the dog. But I need to pack a change of clothes first."

"That animal is not coming in, not for a minute," he repeated.

"Fine, can you watch her for me out here for ten minutes?" Natalie asked.

He frowned at her.

"I'm going to remember this—" she began.

"What? When I need police assistance?" he asked. "You can't do that."

"I was going to say that I will remember this when it's time to sign an extension for my *overpriced* lease," Natalie told him. "Don't think I don't know that I'm paying more than anyone else on my floor."

He at least had the good grace to look a little embarrassed.

She glared at him and he held his hand out for the leash.

"I'll be back in five minutes," she said. "Thank you."

"Don't dilly dally," he grumbled in reply.

She jogged through the courtyard before he could change his mind.

A few minutes later, she returned with a hastily packed bag of clothing and toiletries and was relieved to find Mr. Lancaster still there with Barker Posey.

The dog was sitting politely, smiling up at him.

Mr. Lancaster was smoothing his hand down her head.

"She's nice, isn't she?" Natalie asked, not quite daring to hope.

"She's probably crawling with fleas," her landlord griped, handing over the leash. "Or worse."

"Thanks," Natalie said.

"Don't mention it," he muttered as he headed back inside.

But she could see him peeking out his front window,

probably expecting her to try to sneak the dog into her apartment.

Well, she wasn't going to give him the satisfaction.

She headed toward the street and her phone buzzed in her pocket.

It was a text from Vi.

VIOLET LOCKE:
I have news. Come to 221B.

WELL, that explained exactly nothing.

Still, she had nowhere else to go.

"Come on, Barker Posey," Natalie said. "Let's go for a walk."

After a brisk walk that gave her time to gather herself, she arrived at 221B.

She took a deep breath and rang the bell.

Vi opened the door immediately.

"Took you long enough," she said.

"We walked right over," Natalie said.

"Come on out back," Vi replied, heading down the dark hallway toward the patio.

Natalie couldn't help wondering if Spenser was outside too.

Sure enough, when Vi opened the door, it revealed a lovely scene. Jana was at the picnic table with their landlords, Tony and Micah, pouring out glasses of lemonade.

Hannibal, Fletcher, and Spenser were all shirtless in the yard, tending the rose garden.

Try as she might, Natalie couldn't tear her eyes from Spenser's magnificent, glistening form.

"Quite a sight, isn't it?" Jana asked sympathetically.

Natalie shook her head.

Barker Posey lifted her ears.

That was when Natalie noticed that Micah held a small dog in his lap.

"Oh, I can't believe Maybelle isn't barking," Micah said, delight evident in his voice. "Good girl."

"Is it okay that I have Barker Posey with me?" Natalie asked.

"Of course, and you can let her off the leash," Micah said. "She's very welcome here."

"Why do you have a bag?" Vi asked suspiciously.

Natalie sighed.

"Come sit," Jana said. "Lemonade first, questions later."

"My landlord kicked me out because of the dog," Natalie said, sitting down and accepting the glass. "As soon as we're done catching up, I'm going to find a place to stay, temporarily."

"I wish we had another apartment, honey," Micah told her. "We would be glad to have you and little miss Parker Posey."

"Actually, it's *Barker* Posey," Natalie said. "And thank you. But I'm sure I'll find something."

But she wasn't really sure, it was tough to find a rental with a pet of any kind. And the gentle Saint Bernard was the size of a small pony.

"You will stay with us for tonight," Spenser said, straightening up from the rose bush he was tending to. "So long as this is acceptable to our landlords."

"If you can find room for these two to squeeze in somewhere, they can stay as long as you like," Tony said. "It's nice for Maybelle to have a buddy. Especially now that she's trained enough not to bark at everyone."

They all observed the two dogs, who were lounging under a tree together, tongues lolling out in goofy contentment.

"Thank you," Natalie said, letting out a breath she hadn't realized she'd been holding. "I promise we won't overstay our welcome, but it's getting late, and I was starting to worry a little."

Spenser beamed at her, and her heart did a little flipflop.

Her phone buzzed again, and she saw it was Lila calling from the station.

"Excuse me, I've got to take this," she said, heading inside.

When she reached the dark hallway, she picked up.

"Hey, Lila, any news?" she asked.

"I checked that cam on the mayor's street for last night's footage," Lila said. "Did you know the Peterson's daughter is dating Ed Bachlan?"

"Uh, no," Natalie admitted, wishing she could skip past the gossip.

"Yeah, she totally is, I saw him drop her off at ten and kiss her like he was trying to steal one of her fillings," Lila whispered, clearly loving having this tidbit to share. "The Petersons live next door to Mayor Smalls."

"Any action at the mayor's house?" Natalie asked, anxious to change the subject away from a teenager's social life.

"Oh, yeah," Lila said. "A car turned into his driveway around ten-thirty and left again just before eleven."

"Did you run the plates?" Natalie asked, hoping they were clear enough to read.

"Yes, it was a silver Mercedes, registered to Myra Locke," Lila replied. "Odd for the mayor to want to talk to a lawyer so late at night."

"Yes," Natalie agreed, trying not to stay calm. "Well, it's probably nothing. Thank you for checking. Gotta go."

"Bye now," Lila replied in a disappointed way.

Natalie hung up and stood frozen in the dark hallway, trying to make sense of it all.

But the bottom line was clear.

She had just thrown herself in with Violet Locke and her crew.

But Vi's sister was probably the last person to see Mayor Smalls alive. It didn't mean she was involved, but it definitely complicated matters.

"Everything okay?" Vi's voice cut through the dark hallway.

"Uh, yeah," Natalie replied. "Just someone from work checking on me."

"Nice," Vi said. "I figured I'd carry your bag up for you."

"Thanks," Natalie said.

"Go on out with the others," Vi said. "I'll be down in a sec."

7

SPENSER

Spenser carefully cleaned his gardening shears.

He was making every effort to remain calm and control his physical response. But knowing that Natalie was going to be staying with them made his heart pound as if it were trying to escape his chest.

It was impossible not to imagine being so close with her, talking to her about his feelings, asking her to be his mate.

"Are you alright, brother?" Hannibal asked, approaching him with a sympathetic expression.

"Of course," he replied gruffly.

But somehow, he swallowed the wrong way at the same time, and ended up coughing a little.

Hannibal thumped him on the back as Fletcher loped over with a big grin on his face.

"Have you come to laugh at me too, brother?" Spenser asked.

"Not at all. I have come to sympathize," Fletcher said. "And also a little bit to laugh at you."

Hannibal laughed at that jab. His brothers were much more comfortable with Earth humor than he was.

But Spenser found himself smiling too, in spite of himself.

"We are only amused because we know she cares for you, brother," Fletcher explained. "All will be well."

"How can you say that?" Spenser demanded.

"How can we not say it?" Hannibal replied. "We have seen the way her eyes seek yours. Why don't you tell her how you feel?"

Spenser sighed.

"She is focused on her friend's death. It would be unseemly to speak of it."

Fletcher nodded in agreement.

"Or it might be a comfort," Hannibal suggested.

Spenser thought about that for a moment.

He had never lost a friend.

But he was far from his home, never to return. So he knew something of loss.

"Comfort," he said softly, trying it on for size.

"Give her a chance to say yes," Fletcher suggested. "Tell her she can decide whenever she likes."

"And leave me to suffer," Spenser growled.

"Not deliberately," Hannibal said. "She would never hurt you on purpose. But she might take her time. Would that be so bad?"

Spenser wasn't sure.

"Would anything be worse than right now, when you have no claim on her at all?" Hannibal asked. "Tell her how you feel, before she fears she is misreading her own response to you."

That hit him hard.

"She might not know I feel the bond too?" he asked. "That's impossible."

"It's not impossible at all," Hannibal said solemnly.

"These creatures have trained themselves to ignore even their most basic instincts."

The back door swung open before they could continue their discussion. Natalie wandered out, looking more lost and distracted than before.

Barker Posey loped up to her, nuzzling her hands with her big velvety snout, as if to stop her from dwelling on whatever sad thoughts were racing around her mind.

Natalie smiled at the big dog and ran her hands down Barker's back, then scratched her behind the ear.

"That is exactly where Maybelle likes to be scratched," Spenser said, leaving his brothers behind to move closer, like metal to a magnet.

"Lots of dogs like to be scratched there," Natalie said. "It must be hard for them to reach."

Spenser bent to pat the magnificent creature also.

His hand accidentally brushed Natalie's and he felt a spark of attraction that nearly took his breath away.

He made up his mind on the spot.

He would speak with her about his feelings, and he would do it right away.

"Okay, ready for some news?" Vi announced, stepping back onto the patio.

He fought the urge to bellow with rage at the timing.

Natalie looked up, and Spenser wondered why her expression was slightly wary.

He shrugged it off, assuming his cultural differences were causing him to read her wrong.

They headed for the table and sat down together.

Spenser sat beside Natalie, trying to communicate his love and support to her through the very cells of his body, since he could not talk with her verbally until after Vi had shared her news.

8

NATALIE

Natalie waited, her heart in her mouth.

Spenser joined them and sat down beside her.

She couldn't put her finger on it, but somehow his strong, steady presence gave her a measure of peace.

"There was no EpiPen in the study," Vi began.

"You were barely in there long enough to get a good look around," Natalie said.

"It was plenty of time," Vi said dismissively. "Plenty of time to look for an EpiPen and not find one, and plenty of time to find something very important."

Spenser and the others watched as Vi pulled something out of her pocket with a flourish.

"His phone," Natalie murmured.

"His phone," Vi agreed. "It was under the desk, half under the rug. The police must not have searched very hard."

"They didn't want to investigate at all," Natalie explained.

"That's clear from the bang-up job they did," Vi said, her voice dripping with sarcasm. "Cops."

"Vi," Jana said, elbowing her.

"Present company excluded, of course," Vi added, nodding at Natalie.

"Of course," Natalie agreed, suppressing the desire to snarl. "So what's on the phone?"

"We were hoping you could help with that," Vi said. "Do you have any idea what his passcode might be?"

"That's easy, it would be Barker Posey's birthday," Natalie said.

"Are you sure?" Vi asked.

"Not one hundred percent," Natalie admitted. "But he's the kind of guy to keep his computer password on a sticky note on the monitor. I don't think he would have suddenly become security oriented."

"Makes sense," Vi said. "And I saw that sticky. Your theory checks out."

His work password was BarkerPosey58.

"So what's the dog's birthday?" Vi asked.

"May eighth," Natalie said.

No one asked how she knew, so she was spared the embarrassment of telling them she had attended more than one birthday party for the big dog.

They all watched as Vi typed 0-5-0-8 into the phone.

It unlocked instantly to show a photo of the mayor at his desk, Barker Posey sitting politely by his side.

Natalie sucked in a breath, feeling the pain of his loss all over again.

Harvey Smalls had made some mistakes, but he was a good man. She would miss him for the rest of her life.

"Let's see what's open," Vi said, double-clicking.

She scanned through a fitness app, a mapping app, email, text, and a rundown of phone calls.

"Recent calls," Vi said, clicking.

The most recent was an outgoing call to an unknown number.

Vi made as if to tap on it.

"No," Natalie said quickly. "Don't call from this number."

She slid her own phone out of her pocket and dialed as the others watched, making sure to dial a pre-fix first that would hide her own number from the recipient's caller ID.

She put it on speaker, and placed it on the table.

It rang once, and then someone picked up.

"Myra Croft's office," a young male voice said.

"Wrong number," Natalie said and hung up.

She grabbed the phone and put it back in her pocket, very carefully not speaking or making direct eye contact with anyone.

With luck, she might just pick up on something if anyone here were involved.

"Whoa," Vi said, eyes widening.

"Your sister," Jana said softly.

"No kidding," Vi said. "Let's see what time the call was."

They all watched as she woke the phone, entering the code again.

"Five thirty," Jana said. "Is that still business hours for him?"

"Every hour is a business hour for him," Natalie said neutrally. "But he's often still at town hall at that time."

"I wonder why Myra would have been calling," Vi said. "She's got her hands in a lot of different things for work. But maybe she knows something. I'll go over there in person tomorrow to talk to her."

"Why not call her now?" Natalie asked lightly.

If Vi was stalling for time, it might mean she wanted to warn her sister.

Vi laughed bitterly.

"Because she hates me and would never do anything to help me on purpose. The only way I'll get anything real out of her is to confront her and read her reaction."

Natalie nodded.

It felt like Vi was telling the truth. Vi was good at a lot of things, but subterfuge didn't seem to be one of them. Though she was incredibly clever…

"So what other clues were there?" Jana asked. "Besides the phone?"

"Did you notice the lemon squares?" Vi asked Natalie.

"Yeah, I saw there were treats on his desk," Natalie said.

"Those weren't just treats," Vi said. "Those were Rose Wilkinson's lemon squares."

Rose Wilkinson's lemon squares were famous in the little town. She made them for every PTA gathering and town council meeting. She made them for the bake sale to support the Stargazer Firefighters and Emergency Worker's Fund too. That was where Natalie had developed a taste for them.

Mayor Smalls loved Rose's lemon squares too. They were a staple of his beloved Stargazer.

"That's funny," Natalie said.

"What?" Vi asked.

"Well, Rose's lemon squares don't have nuts in them," Natalie said.

"How do you know?" Vi asked.

"Because I've seen him eat them before," Natalie said. "He loves them. They're his go-to at the bake sales because it's the one thing he doesn't have to ask the recipe for before he eats it."

"There was no other food in that room," Vi said.

"Are we sure those were Rose's lemon squares?" Jana ventured. "Maybe someone else made similar ones?"

"Who would put nuts in a lemon square?" Vi asked disdainfully. "That's just disgusting."

Jana lifted her hands in surrender.

"Unless that someone wanted to kill the mayor, and knew he wouldn't question the ingredients," Vi mused.

Natalie's eyebrows shot up.

Rose Wilkinson was one of the nicest ladies in town. The idea of her killing the mayor was preposterous, at best.

A good cop takes nothing at face value, she reminded herself. *A good cop checks out every lead.*

"If nothing else, maybe she saw something when she dropped off the squares," Natalie suggested. "Let's go see her."

Vi nodded, a glimmer of respect in her eyes.

Natalie couldn't help feeling grateful to have someone likeminded and sharp to bounce around ideas with.

"I will come too," Spenser said, a growl of protection in his deep voice.

Natalie tried to ignore what the sound did to her. The last thing she needed was that kind of distraction.

"Of course," Vi said. "We're all going. Come on."

9

SPENSER

Spenser sat beside Natalie in the old ice cream truck, trying to focus on their goal.

But it was hard not to feast his eyes on her beautiful face, teasingly illuminated by street lights and cast into darkness again at intervals.

For her part, Natalie looked nervous. She drummed her fingers on her thigh as if they could not reach their destination fast enough.

The details of the problem at hand were complicated, but Spenser understood that there was some possibility that the woman they were visiting had secretly added nuts to a recipe as a way of poisoning the mayor.

It also seemed that none of them believed she would do such a thing.

Which made it odd that Natalie would feel so nervous. Even if she was the culprit, this woman was unlikely to use force against them for confronting her, in any case.

Since joining Vi's extended family, Spenser had read a bit about detectives and detective work. The profile for a poisoner was different from that of a violent killer.

He wanted to remind Natalie of this, but since she was a police officer, he was sure she already knew.

Which meant her nervousness was not about the potential poisoner, but about something else.

There must be something about the case that was escaping him.

"Here we are," Vi announced, pulling up in front of a small brick house.

The six of them piled out of the car. Tony and Micah had offered to keep an eye on Barker Posey while they were out, and Natalie had accepted gratefully.

Spenser stood on the sidewalk at Natalie's side, Fletcher, Jana, and Hannibal beside them.

They all watched as Vi rang the bell.

A moment later, the door opened.

"Oh, hello," a tiny older lady said, looking around at the group gathered in front of her house in surprise. "Is everything alright?"

"Yes, Miss Wilkinson," Vi said. "But we'd like to ask you about something. Would that be okay?"

"Of course, dear, but you can call me Rose," Rose said.

"Thank you, Rose," Vi replied. "Come on, guys."

Spenser followed closely behind Natalie into the little house.

It was dim inside, but he could make out a flowery sofa and a small table. Two spindly chairs were opposite the sofa.

"Let's go into the dining room," Rose suggested. "There are enough seats for everyone there."

They followed her into the next room. Sure enough there was a large table with ten chairs. They seated themselves.

"May I offer you something to eat or drink?" Rose asked.

Hannibal opened his mouth and lifted his hand as if to ask for a snack and Vi smacked his hand back down.

"We're fine," Vi said firmly. "We just ate."

"So what did you want to ask me about?" Rose asked, pulling out a chair and lowering herself carefully into it.

"It's the mayor," Vi said. "Do you know what happened to him?"

"No," Rose said, leaning forward. "Is he okay?"

Jana bit her lip.

"It's not common knowledge yet," Vi said. "But no, he's not. He passed away in his home last night."

Rose looked aghast. "Oh no," she moaned. "Poor Mayor Smalls."

"Yes," Vi said. "It was unexpected."

"What happened to him?" Rose asked, looking very upset.

Spenser was beginning to feel that maybe they had made a mistake coming here.

"He had an allergic reaction," Vi said.

"To what?" Rose asked. "I didn't know he had an allergy."

"You didn't?" Vi asked.

Rose shook her head.

"He was allergic to nuts," Natalie said quietly.

Spenser watched the woman's face seem to crumble and fall to pieces. She lowered her face into her hands and sobbed like a child.

"Rose?" Vi said.

Jana pulled a tissue out of her purse and handed it over.

Rose took it and blew her nose like a trumpet.

"It's all my fault," she said simply.

"What do you mean?" Vi asked.

"My lemon squares," Rose said, and blew her nose again.

"There are no nuts in a lemon square," Vi said.

"There didn't used to be," Rose agreed tearfully. "But my son had a heart scare last year and he's trying to eat healthier. So I've been working on a new recipe that everyone can enjoy."

Some of those words didn't make sense to Spenser. He looked to Natalie, who was nodding slowly.

"My new lemon square recipe is low-carb," Rose said sadly. "I used erythritol for the filling, and almond flour for the crust. My son said he can't taste the difference."

"My God," Vi breathed.

"I dropped off a batch for the mayor yesterday," Rose went on. "He always says how much he likes them at the bake sale. I figured he could use some cheering up after... everything that happened. I meant to tell him they were guilt-free, but he wasn't home when I dropped them off."

Rose's lower lip trembled again, and she closed her eyes, tears streaming down her wrinkled cheeks. "I'm so sorry," she whispered.

"You did nothing wrong," Jana told her immediately. "You didn't know he had an allergy. It was kind of you to bring him a treat."

Vi scowled at Jana, as if she didn't want anyone to sympathize.

But Spenser couldn't imagine this poor woman had done anything to harm the mayor on purpose.

"The mayor knows... *knew* he needed to check ingredients and keep an EpiPen near at all times," Natalie added. "We're not sure why he didn't have one yesterday, but we're looking into it. Thank you for allowing us into your home and for talking with us."

"Can I call your son for you?" Jana asked. "Do you have his number?"

Rose was still sniffling. She and Jana headed into the kitchen to make the call.

Spenser thought this was a fine idea. The poor lady should not be left alone and upset.

"Well that was a dead end," Vi said as soon as they were out of earshot.

"We know where the nuts came from, at least," Natalie said.

Vi nodded once.

"I hope you don't think this is the end of the investigation," Natalie said. "I still don't believe for a minute he would be without an EpiPen in reach. Something fishy is going on."

Spenser held his breath, hoping Vi would not deny his mate her opportunity to keep searching for answers.

"Agreed," Vi said. "I guess we'll head home once her son gets here. I need to think on this."

10

SPENSER

Back at 221B, Spenser led the way to the second-floor landing, with Natalie in tow.

"Are you sure this isn't an imposition?" Natalie asked. "I don't want to crowd you and your brothers."

"Not at all," Spenser said. "Ever since my brothers met their mates, I've been spending a lot of time alone in the apartment. They come up a lot during the day, but I think it's mostly because they do not wish for me to be lonely."

Belatedly, he realized that what he had shared might sound like a ploy for sympathy. He hadn't meant it that way.

Natalie merely nodded without fawning over him, which made him instantly grateful.

"Well, that works out well for Barker Posey and me," she said.

He opened the door and the big dog leapt up from her position on the sofa and trotted over to meet them.

"Hi, girl," Natalie said, crouching down to greet the dog.

For an instant, Spenser allowed himself to imagine this as his life - a kind mate, an interesting pet, the sense of home he felt walking in this door with Natalie.

Then he shook his head and tried to focus.

He had to talk to her first.

She was smiling as the dog kissed her by licking her cheek.

He was very lucky that the dog was here, helping her to feel more at peace and less worried about what had happened to Mayor Smalls.

He went into the kitchen and put the water on for tea.

Dr. Bhimani had prepared tea for the brothers whenever there was something important to talk about. The ritual always calmed him.

A few minutes later, Natalie poked her head in.

"Need some help?" she asked.

His heart was warmed.

Mates helped each other. She already had the instinct to honor their bond, even if they hadn't said the words yet.

"Yes, please," he replied. "Would you choose two mugs for us? I thought we could drink some tea and talk."

"That sounds amazing," Natalie said.

They bustled around the kitchen together for a few minutes. The room was small enough that she occasionally brushed up against him.

Each time, he closed his eyes and prayed for the strength to talk with her patiently instead of turning around to grab her and tell her with his body what he knew she needed to hear in words.

At last they sat down at the table, steaming mugs before them.

"Did you want to talk about the case?" Natalie asked. "Did you notice something?"

He shook his head and pressed his lips together, trying to find a way to begin.

She placed her hand on his.

He closed his eyes and let the emotions flood his body. Her touch made everything right.

He opened his eyes to see her looking at their hands.

"There is something between us," he said to her without even having to think about his words. "Do you understand what it is?"

"I think so," she said, her voice soft and low. "But will you explain anyway?"

"My brothers and I, we are here for one reason," he told her. "And though we fill our days with other things, that reason looms for me."

She nodded, giving him time.

"I have done my best to find a mate, going to places where I might find a kindred spirit, a woman who might want someone like me," he said gruffly, feeling a little embarrassed. "But I have never once felt with anyone the way I feel when I am with you."

She squeezed his hand.

"I am yours," he said simply. "If you will have me."

She took a deep breath and looked up at him, her eyes luminous. For a moment, he allowed himself to hope.

"What does it mean if we're... mates?" she asked.

"It means everything," he told her. "It means we love each other. It means I will protect you, even if to do so is to sacrifice myself. It means we will always be honest with each other, no matter what."

Her expression changed.

It was as if she were suddenly closed to him, cold and distant.

"Natalie, what is it?" he asked. "What have I done wrong?"

"Nothing," she said, smiling.

The expression was gone from her face now. But he knew what he had seen.

"You do not wish to be bonded so completely to another," he guessed.

She removed her hand from his and stood up.

He watched, willing himself not to leap up after her.

She paced to one end of the small room and back again. At last she stopped and leaned against the counter by the sink.

"Spenser, everything you've proposed sounds incredible," she said. "It's everything I could ever ask for in a relationship."

He smiled at her encouragingly.

"But right now," she went on, "I'm focused on the mayor's death. I can't promise to put you first when I have a case to solve that's so personal."

This did not make sense to him. Would he not help her solve it?

"I am pledging you my loyalty," he told her. "I will do anything to help you."

"That means the world to me," she told him, her voice breaking. "Do you think you could give me some time?"

He nodded, not trusting himself to speak for fear that he would beg her for what she would not give freely tonight.

"Thank you," she said softly, pressing her hand to her mouth, clearly trying to hold back her tears.

He was on his feet before he knew what was happening, pulling her into his arms, holding her close to comfort her.

She seemed to melt into his embrace.

He soaked her in, trying to memorize the softness of her curves, the cinnamon scent of her hair.

She pulled back as he loosened his hold slightly, and

then she went up on her toes and slid her hands around his neck, pressing her lips to his.

Lightning flashed behind his eyelids as a thunderstorm gathered in his chest. She had awoken something in him, a passion akin to fury, strong as a force of nature.

He swept her up in his arms, carrying her to his room.

She clung to him, as if she were dying to surrender.

He placed her gently on the ground just in front of the bed.

She reached under the hem of his t-shirt.

He shivered at the sensation of her warm hands, sliding the material up until they had to break their contact for him to pull it over his head.

She waited for him to throw it to the floor, then her hands were at his fly, clever fingers sliding against the button.

"No," he whispered, taking both her hands in one of his.

"I want—" she began.

He stopped her with another kiss, feeding on her mouth as if he might never stop.

When she gave up on talking, he slipped his hands under her shirt, sliding it up just as she had done to him.

When they pulled apart to get it all the way off, he saw that she was wearing a shimmering undergarment which lifted her breasts, yet also mostly bared them to him.

He was breathless for a moment, gazing down at her.

"You are so beautiful," he told her.

She took his hand and placed it on her breast.

He cupped it reverently, smoothing his thumb over her nipple, still encased in satin.

She sighed and he felt the nipple harden and press against the fabric, aching for his touch.

An answering ache from his groin took his breath away a

second time. He lowered his face to brush the tops of her breasts hungrily with his lips.

Natalie arched her back, as if begging for closer contact.

He reached around behind her, knowing he could not remove her undergarments as smoothly as the men in the spy movies, but hoping that he would not struggle so much as the boys in the college comedies.

Natalie put the matter to rest by undoing the garment herself and letting it slide down her arms to the ground.

He tugged open the button on her jeans and slid the zipper down.

She helped him drag down her jeans and panties, shimmying out of them in a way that made her soft curves jiggle most pleasantly.

At last, she stood before him, naked. The moonlight glowed in her eyes and made her hair shine onyx like the glass cliffs of Aerie.

"Spenser," she whispered, reaching for his jeans again.

"Not yet," he told her, though his body raged and stormed for her touch.

She frowned, but when he leaned in to kiss her, she melted into his arms again.

11

NATALIE

Natalie lost herself in Spenser's kiss.

Whatever she had told herself about holding off, not allowing him to become her mate yet - it all felt impossible now.

How could she resist this pull?

Why had she ever wanted to in the first place?

She couldn't remember, couldn't imagine anything except the gentleness of his big hands, the taste of his tongue.

She lay back on the bed, the pillowcase cool beneath her head, Spenser's body warm and hard against hers.

She twined her arms around his neck, wrapped her legs around his waist, trying to pull him closer, to assimilate him if she could.

He fed on her mouth, his kisses slow and passionate, sending her into madness.

She slid a hand down to cup his jaw.

He pulled away from her mouth to kiss her palm and run his tongue down her fingers.

Natalie closed her eyes, felt a shiver of lightning in her veins.

He kissed her neck, nuzzling his way down between her breasts. When he lashed a nipple with his tongue she cried out, and he pulled back.

"Does it hurt?" he asked, concern marring his handsome face.

"No, it feels good, so good," she whispered, her back arching of its own accord, breasts dancing to be back in his mouth.

He smiled and lowered his face slowly to meet her chest, flicking her nipple again with his tongue, mimicking the motion on her other nipple with his thumb.

She let her head fall back on the pillow and managed not to scream in frustration when he abandoned her breasts too soon to kiss his way down her belly.

She froze when he pressed her thighs apart.

He stopped to look up at her, a question in his eyes.

"I-I don't like that," she murmured.

"You don't want me to kiss you there?" he asked, licking his lips.

She saw the movement of his tongue against that wickedly handsome mouth and her hips lifted slightly of their own accord.

"I will not if you do not wish it," he told her. "But if you let me try, I will stop at once if I do not please you."

She opened her mouth and closed it again. All language was gone, gone from her brain. There was only Spenser and that mouth and those hands...

She nodded once.

He nodded back, as if they had made a solemn pact.

She closed her eyes and tried not to think about it. A boyfriend or two had tried this on her before. One was too rough, another too gentle. And the whole thing made her self-conscious.

Then Spenser's mouth was on her and she forgot every experience she'd ever had.

Natalie clutched the sheets, every nerve ending tingling as he pushed her closer and closer to the edge.

He moaned against her hungrily, the vibration pushing her further, faster.

Suddenly, a rainbow of sensation burst through the storm, carrying her up, up, up, and then bursting her open with ecstasy.

Natalie lost track of her own sounds as she felt herself splinter into a thousand pieces.

Finally, the last of her shivers ceased and she felt Spenser crawling up to her, holding her, pulling her onto his chest.

She nuzzled the place where his neck met his shoulder and slid her hand lazily down his abs to find what she wanted.

But he stopped her hand again.

"Sleep, my beautiful one," he murmured, holding her close. "Tonight I will hold you. Tomorrow, when the air is clear, we may claim each other if we choose."

And though she could feel the longing radiating from his big body, she let him move her hand away so he could hold her.

Somehow, her eyes were already heavy with sleep.

And everything just felt so right. She was sure they would sort it all out in the morning.

12

NATALIE

Natalie awoke feeling warm and contented.

She stretched and found strong arms around her.

Spenser.

Yes, it had all been real. The big man was sleeping beside her, a peaceful expression on his beautiful features.

She slid out of his arms as slowly and carefully as she could, and turned back to observe him.

A little sunlight from the window gave him an otherworldly glow, and for a moment she was mesmerized.

This man was her mate. She could feel the bond between them even now, pulling her back into his arms.

She closed her eyes and tried to remind herself why that was a bad idea.

She should have had more self-control last night. She had Spenser to thank for the fact that she wasn't already in too deep. At least he had showed a little restraint.

She grabbed her bag and tiptoed out of the room, headed for the shower.

Barker Posey was waiting in the living room, her tail thumping the sofa.

Natalie dropped her backpack, grabbed the dog's leash, and headed for the door. Barker Posey joined her with a grateful smile, and they headed downstairs. She was going to have to get used to life with a canine companion.

The dawn sky was pink over Stargazer. Barker Posey obligingly went about her business as Natalie looked around at the sleepy little town.

It seemed unfair that anything bad could ever happen here among the sweet little houses and busy downtown.

When they stepped back into the apartment, Barker Posey went right for the sofa while Natalie grabbed her bag again and headed into the bathroom for a quick shower.

Slipping under the steamy water allowed her to focus on her mission once more.

I will find out what happened to Harvey Smalls.

And to do that, I have to thoroughly investigate Myra Croft. Even though she is Vi's sister.

The gang already knew that there had been a phone call with Croft's office the night of the mayor's death.

But they didn't know what Natalie did, that Myra's car had been spotted heading in and out of the mayor's driveway the night he died.

If she told them, they would hate her.

And Vi planned to confront Myra today anyway.

Natalie planned to tag along on that mission and glean all she could. Maybe it would turn out to be a coincidence.

But if Myra Croft was guilty, Natalie would stop at nothing to put her behind bars.

Even if there was no love lost between Vi and Myra, they were family. In Natalie's experience that counted for a lot.

Accusing Myra was bound to piss Vi off, and possibly alienate the rest of her crew.

And that could mean losing Spenser.

Natalie dunked her head under the shower nozzle, as if the hot water could wash away the bothersome thoughts.

She emerged a few minutes later, felling a little more relaxed, and then dressed hastily from the clothing in her backpack.

Good smells and happy sounds greeted her from the kitchen.

"Are you singing a Cyndi Lauper song?" she asked as she joined Spenser by the stove.

He was making lumpy pancakes and humming like a canary.

"Jana will play Cyndi in a play in New York," Spenser explained. "She practices a lot, and then the songs get stuck in everyone's heads. This song was in one of the movies my brothers and I used to learn about human culture."

Natalie smiled picturing the big men watching light-hearted movies about girls in dance competitions.

"Vi has already sent Hannibal to tell me that we must meet them downstairs in half an hour," he went on. "We're going to confront her sister."

"All of us?" Natalie asked.

"Yes, of course," Spenser said. "She wants as many eyes on Myra and her office as possible."

That was encouraging.

"You eat," Spenser told her, sliding a plate in front of her and turning off the stove. "I'm going to shower, then we'll go."

"Thank you," she said, accepting the stack of lumpy pancakes.

He kissed the top of her head and a shiver ran through her.

But she managed not to grab and kiss him.

As he headed for the bathroom, she took a tiny bite of the pancakes.

They were warm and delicious. They tasted like home.

She finished them while Spenser got ready, then they headed out to meet the others.

Half an hour later, the six friends hopped out of the van at Myra's office.

Vi headed for the door and they all trailed after her.

"May I help you?" an assistant with a bored expression on his face asked from behind a mahogany desk.

"We're here to see Myra," Vi said crisply, heading right to the closed door on the right.

"You don't have an appointment," the assistant said, his expression shifting quickly from bored to anxious.

But it was too late, Vi had already flung open the door and headed inside. The others followed, leaving the assistant looking flabbergasted. Natalie had to give him credit. He really had a range.

"What a surprise," Myra Croft said in a crystal-clear deadpan voice.

Natalie made it in far enough to see that Vi's sister was still sitting behind her desk. Myra's body was relaxed, and she gazed indolently at them like a lazy cat.

But Natalie sensed the energy of a caged tiger behind those eyes.

"Why did you call the mayor the night before last?" Vi demanded.

"I heard about that," Myra responded. "Such a tragedy."

It made sense. Natalie had been busy, but the news of the mayor's death would be public knowledge by now.

"And?" Vi urged, not letting her sister dodge the question.

"Client business is confidential," Myra replied crisply. "Though I suppose you would know nothing about that in your line of work." Myra's nose wrinkled delicately in distaste.

Natalie pictured steam coming out of Vi's ears and the little detective losing her cool.

"So you deny making the call?" Vi asked coolly, ignoring her sister's baiting. "You've had no personal or professional business with the mayor in the last forty-eight hours?"

Myra stood and walked partly around her desk to face her sister. "I'm under no obligation to answer to you," she said. "You're not a police officer."

"But I am," Natalie offered.

Myra backed up slightly, surprising Natalie. She hadn't pictured Myra Croft backing off, ever.

"Then arrest me," Myra said, arching one eyebrow.

For so many reasons, Natalie couldn't do that.

"I thought not," Myra smirked. "Get out of my office before I file a formal complaint."

"Someone is going to question you about that phone call," Vi said calmly. "Wouldn't you rather it was us?"

Myra's face went still for an instant.

"*Kendall, get them out of here,*" she yelled.

The assistant, looking even more horrified than before, scuttled in and glanced around.

He was young, with a slight build, and he was currently surrounded by three massive, muscle-bound men and three angry women. Natalie wondered exactly what Myra expected him to do.

"Don't bother, Kendall," Vi said. "We're going."

The young assistant stepped aside.

Myra Croft stayed right where she was, watching them go, an icy expression in her eyes.

Ten minutes later, the gang was settled at the picnic table, back in their own backyard.

"It's a shame that was a bust," Jana said, shaking her head.

"What are you talking about?" Vi laughed. "That wasn't a bust at all."

Natalie leaned forward, curious as to what Vi had seen that had given her new information.

"What on earth did you learn from that?" Jana asked.

"You can't listen to anything she says," Vi explained. "That way madness lies. The only reason she ever opens her mouth is to elicit a response. When it comes to Myra, you have to pay attention to what she does, not what she says."

"What did she do?" Hannibal asked, amazed. "I thought all she did was talk."

Vi shook her head. "Did you see what she did when I brought up the mayor?"

Everyone shook their heads.

"She stood up," Natalie said.

"Yes, thank god, someone else with a decent pair of eyes," Vi said. "She stood up, but that wasn't all."

Vi looked at Natalie expectantly.

"Well, she moved toward you, to talk," Natalie offered, trying to picture Myra's movements in her mind.

"It might have looked that way, but that wasn't what was really happening," Vi said. "Even Myra herself may have consciously thought she was standing in order to confront me. But I know what she was really doing."

"Come on, Vi, tell us," Jana urged her.

"She was moving her body between us and the thing she

didn't want us to know about," Vi said. "She was probably doing it subconsciously, but she was doing it."

"That's why she stepped back from me," Natalie said, realizing.

"Myra never steps down from a confrontation," Vi said. "She was falling back to protect something."

"What was she protecting?" Jana asked.

But Natalie could see it now, the thing that was hidden from her view a moment after she began to speak.

"The wall safe," Natalie said.

"Bingo," Vi said, grinning at her.

"What safe?" Jana asked, looking back and forth between them. "I didn't see a safe."

"Me neither. But there must be one behind the painting," Natalie explained. "That's a common spot for a safe."

"Ah," Hannibal said.

"So all we have to do is check out the safe, and we'll know what's up with her," Vi said, as though that would be the simplest thing to do.

"How in the world are we supposed to get into that safe?" Jana asked, echoing Natalie's doubts.

"That's the hard part," Vi admitted.

Spenser cleared his throat.

They all turned to him.

"Have I ever told you about my gift?" he asked.

Natalie looked at the other two women, shaking their heads.

Hannibal gave Spenser an almost imperceptible nod.

"We are not supposed to share our gift, except with our bonded mates," Spenser said. "But given the circumstances..."

He glanced up at Natalie and his cheeks were suddenly flushed.

She resisted the urge to take his hand, instead she nodded encouragingly.

"Each of us seems to have brought with us a gift that might be considered supernatural to the residents of Earth," he explained. "We believe it ties to our character and to our time on Aerie. We do not share our gifts, as we do not want to frighten humans. Anything that makes us seem less human only hurts our mission."

"We'll be fine, Spenser," Natalie said in a steady voice that belied her twisting insides.

"I have a gift you might call... minor telekinesis," he said. "I can call things to me with my mind, small things, non-living things."

"That's amazing," Natalie breathed.

"So what did you swipe?" Vi asked, instantly practical.

He lifted something for them to see.

It was a small envelope, marked *Safety Deposit Box*

Vi took it from him and slid her finger under the flap to open it, dumping the contents on the table between them.

A plastic keycard fell onto the table. The words *SAFE-T-STOR Emergency Access* were printed across the top.

"It's the back-up access to her wall safe," Vi breathed.

"I do not like to steal things," Spenser said solemnly, looking a little ashamed. "But I had a sudden sense that it might be important, since our talking wasn't going anywhere."

"You did the right thing," Natalie told him. "That was a good instinct."

He smiled down at her in relief, looking perfectly content at her words.

She was struck by the irony of his incredible special ability and massive physical prowess, set against his child-like innocence.

Spenser was both charming and dangerous.

Being his mate would be a huge responsibility.

She shook her head to clear it. She could worry about all that later. For now they had to solve their case.

"So gang, are we ready for another round of breaking and entering?" Vi asked cheerfully.

Another round?

Natalie fought her instincts and decided it was better not to ask.

13

SPENSER

A few hours later, Spenser huddled in the back of the van with Natalie and Vi. He was feeling a little nervous, but also excited to be included in the group caper, especially since Natalie was involved.

"Are you sure it's a good idea to sneak in there in the middle of the day?" Natalie asked.

"Myra goes to Hot Pilates every day during her lunch break. It's the only regular part of her schedule," Vi said firmly. "Her ex-husband once accused her of having a beer belly, and it completely traumatized her. She never misses a day - never."

"Funny, she doesn't strike me as the beer type," Natalie mused.

"Oh, she isn't," Vi said. "And as far as I can tell, her stomach is as normal as every other part of her. But Myra's a control freak. So lunchtime is the exact right time for a visit. Besides, if you get caught, you can just say you left something behind earlier. You know, drop your phone on the floor and then pretend to find it."

Vi was clearly more skilled at this type of thing

than the rest of them. Spenser wasn't very good at lying. And he didn't like the way it made him feel when he tried. So he usually just tried to avoid it if he could.

"So what do we do now?" Natalie asked.

"First, we're going to get her office back door key," Vi said. "It will be in her gym locker. Then we just have to get to her office and back before her one-hour class is over. Easy-peasy."

That did not sound easy-peasy to Spenser.

Natalie let out a long breath, and he realized with relief that she must feel the same.

"Look," Vi hissed nodding

They all watched as Myra got into her car and adjusted the seat and mirrors, checked her hair, and pulled out of her parking spot.

Vi waited for a moment after her sister pulled out and then pulled the ice cream truck out to follow at a reasonable distance.

"Why did we have to follow her?" Natalie asked. "We know where she's going."

"She's got two different gym memberships," Vi explained. "She mixes it up so that no one at either place realizes what a freak she is."

Natalie nodded and they drove on in silence, at last rounding the corner and pulling into the lot of the Fitness Planet.

Now that the mission was before him, Spenser was suddenly more apprehensive.

Was it really wise to take something from Myra, then break into her office?

But Vi was already out of the van, waiting for them at the glass doors of the exercise studio.

Natalie looked at Spenser and shrugged, then they both headed to join their friend.

"I'll stand outside the locker room so I can distract anyone trying to get in," Vi said. "The class will start in about two minutes and forty seconds, so we should wait out here until then. After that, you should be home free."

"Aren't people sometimes a few minutes late?" Natalie asked. "She could still be in the changing room."

"Not for Hot Pilates," Vi said, as if it were obvious. "This is a waiting-room only class for serious exercise seekers."

Natalie blinked at her.

"At least that's what it says on the web page," Vi confided. "No lateness will be tolerated. Doors lock at noon. Myra's locker number will be 12."

"How do you know?" Natalie asked.

"It's her lucky number," Vi said. "She's super weird about it."

Spenser knew that Vi had some superstitions of her own, but he thought it was probably best not to mention it.

"What do you think she would do if she caught us taking something from her?" Natalie asked.

It was the same question Spenser had.

"Let's not find out," Vi said, nodding at her watch and pushing open the door to the gym.

They headed in, and the woman at the desk waved.

Vi went straight over and began asking long, boring questions that would require very detailed answers.

Natalie pointed to the ladies' room and the lady at the desk nodded.

As soon as she was focused on Vi again, Natalie grabbed Spenser's hand and dragged him into a door marked *Changing Room - Femmes*.

They scanned the room.

He spotted locker #12 and ran for it.

"Shit," Natalie said when she noticed the combination lock. "How did we not plan for this?"

But Spenser merely took the lock in his hand, and used his gift to ask all the little tumblers inside to line up neatly.

Natalie's eyes opened wide as the lock popped open.

"Wow," she said appreciatively, then hesitated for a second. "If you can do that, then why are we here to steal a key in the first place?"

"Keyed locks are different," he explained. "Too many moving parts."

He'd tried to practice on one of the doors back at the lab, but holding all those little pieces in the perfect position was just too much. Combination locks were easy compared to that. Just one thing to move at time, and all the pieces stayed exactly where you left them.

"I guess you could have a pretty promising career as a bicycle thief," Natalie joked as she opened the locker and pawed through Myra's belongings.

Spenser felt a wave of relief. He'd been so conditioned to keep his gift hidden, that he'd been nervous about finally using it in front of anyone. But Natalie didn't seem to mind. In fact, she seemed to find it pretty impressive.

Natalie pulled a huge keychain from Myra's purse. The sheer number of keys was overwhelming. He wondered how they would even have time to test them all.

But Natalie turned them in her hands, examining the heads, each of which had a tiny sticker label. Myra might be even more organized than Vi.

"Got it," she whispered victoriously.

He closed his eyes and called on his power to separate the key from the ring.

"So if we don't get it back in time all the keys aren't all

missing," he explained. "Maybe she'll just think it fell off somehow."

"Great idea," Natalie said, her beautiful face breaking into a big smile.

He resisted the impulse to kiss her and instead moved back toward the entry door.

She followed him and they listened before opening, but no sound penetrated the wooden frame.

Natalie opened the door to find Vi on the other side, studying a schedule.

"We're good?" Vi asked.

"We're good," Natalie echoed.

Spenser couldn't help but notice how well the two were getting along. It was hard not to picture what a great team they would all make if Natalie accepted him fully and became part of the group.

The ride back to Myra's office was quiet and tense.

Spenser imagined they were all picturing the task ahead, envisioning what would happen if they succeeded and what could happen if they failed.

For a moment, he nearly regretted swiping the envelope in the first place.

But then he thought of his mate's mourning over her lost friend and knew he would do what he had to do, over and over again, if it brought her some measure of relief.

Vi turned the truck into the alleyway behind Myra's office, then pulled up behind a parking area that said PRIVATE PARKING on a small sign in neat lettering.

"You'll have to scale the fence to get to the little deck," Vi said. "That's the back door to her office."

Natalie was already climbing out of the van, so Spenser hurried to follow her.

He observed the large fence and wondered how he could get her over it.

But before he could come up with a plan, she was running, pulling herself up and over easily, as if it were just for fun.

He followed, impressed by his capable mate.

They climbed the two steps up to the wooden deck and Natalie used the key they had stolen to open the back door into Myra's office.

Natalie placed a finger to her lips and pulled the door open slowly. They went in and she pulled it almost all the way shut behind them, but didn't close the latch.

Spenser heard a voice and froze in place.

Then he realized it was Myra's assistant on the phone in the lobby just outside. He must not take his lunch break at the same time that she did.

It was good that the man was on the phone, hopefully it meant he was distracted enough not to notice a stray noise or two from this room.

Natalie wasn't wasting any time. She had already moved to the painting, and was in the process of lifting it off the wall. Sure enough, there was a wall safe behind it, just as they had suspected.

Spenser handed Natalie the key card and watched as she swiped it down the side of the safe.

The door made a loud click-pop sound and swung open.

The two of them froze, but the phone call in the lobby droned on, they hadn't been heard.

Inside the safe was a single file.

Natalie grabbed it and spread the contents hastily along the floor behind Myra's desk. Then she pulled out her phone and began photographing each image, starting with the one on the left.

After she took each photo, Spenser grabbed the sheet and laid it upside down on one side of the folder.

Out in the lobby, Myra's assistant was laughing at something the caller had said.

Natalie seemed to redouble her efforts.

Spenser wondered if funny things happened at the end of phone calls.

Sure enough, as he placed the last page back inside the folder the sounds from the lobby ended.

Natalie took the file and put it back in the safe.

It closed with another loud click and pop.

Natalie moved quickly to hang the picture back over it.

"Myra?" the assistant's voice called from the lobby.

Natalie grabbed Spenser's hand and dragged him under the desk.

"Are you there?" the assistant asked.

The door opened and Spenser closed his eyes, hoping they wouldn't be spotted.

"Weird," the assistant said.

Spenser opened his eyes and listened to the footsteps heading toward the desk.

But they passed by, then went to the door that led to the deck.

"Must have blown open," the assistant said to himself.

A moment later the door to the lobby closed and they were alone once more.

Spenser moved as if to run for the door to the deck, but Natalie stopped him with a touch.

They waited in silence and Spenser began to wonder how much time had passed. His heart pounded madly, and he began to think about what he could do if the man came back in.

If he jumped out and surrendered himself it might allow Natalie an opportunity to get away. This was probably best.

Natalie had gotten out her phone, she was typing in a number.

It was an odd time to make a telephone call. He might have expected her to text Vi for help, but a phone call seemed unnecessarily noisy.

The sound of a phone ringing carried to them from the lobby.

"Myra Croft's office," the assistant's voice rang out from the next room and echoed in the phone in her hand.

Natalie tapped mute on the screen and dragged Spenser bodily out from under the desk.

"Hello?" the assistant said.

A moment later they were out the door, leaping off the deck, running for the fence.

When they landed on the other side, Natalie hung up the call.

"Natalie," Spenser said, amazed at her ingenuity.

She grinned at him.

"What are you guys standing around smiling about?" Vi demanded. "Get in, get in, before someone sees us."

They got into the van and it was the most natural thing in the world for Spenser to throw an arm around his incredible mate and kiss the top of her head.

She leaned in, warming his heart with the proof that she craved his touch as well.

14

NATALIE

Natalie watched as Vi spread papers across the floor.

Jana had printed out the photos Natalie had taken of Myra's file to make the pages easier to study.

Now the six of them huddled around the patterned wool rug in Vi and Jana's living room, watching Vi drink in the contents of the documents like a movie vampire crouched over a corpse.

"My God," she murmured, swiping one page out of the way and snatching another one.

From what Natalie could tell, there were basically two types of documents.

Some were plot maps, and others appeared to be sale documents and titles. None of it seemed like unusual stuff to find in an attorney's office.

On her own, Natalie would certainly have studied them carefully, leaving no door unopened. But Vi was devouring them, as if each fresh page only made her more ravenous for the next.

Natalie stayed out of the line of fire, knowing she would

have her chance to look over everything as soon as Vi was finished.

"Okay," Vi said at last, sitting back on her heels. "Okay, wow."

"So what are we looking at?" Jana asked.

"There's a reason these were kept as hard copies in a safe, and not stored electronically on Myra's hard drive," Vi began. "I knew as soon as Natalie told us that what she and Spenser found was paperwork, that this had to be serious."

Natalie sat back against the sofa, realizing this was going to take a moment.

Vi had a great point though. In this day and age, important documents were generally stored under password in the cloud so they couldn't be lost.

"Myra didn't want anyone seeing these or connecting these transactions to her," Vi went on.

"What transactions?" Jana asked.

"Land purchases," Vi said, confirming Natalie's suspicion. "It looks like a corporation called Kendra Z. Bose, Inc. has been buying up land on the northwest side of town and Myra's been handling the paperwork."

"You mean out where we found the dogs?" Jana asked.

"Yes," Vi replied. "It's a rural area, and the land there is fairly cheap. The bulk of it honestly can't even be built on, and there's no farming on most of it because it's all granite crags and floodplain."

"What do they want with that land?" Natalie asked.

"That's the thing," Vi said. "Typically, with a land purchase like this you see contingencies for zoning. No one wants to buy a chunk of land and find out they can't build what they had in mind on it."

Natalie nodded, that made sense.

"But there is nothing like that here," Vi continued. "And

this isn't just one land purchase. It's multiple parcels, big and small."

"So why do they want it?" Jana asked.

"I'm not sure," Vi admitted. "But there's a map here that looks like it might be for utilities or something going in. But that doesn't make sense, since a utility company can take an easement for free, even if they don't own the land. So they wouldn't have to buy it all up. And this company name isn't a utility anyway, at least not a local one."

"I can't find anything about Kendra Bose," Jana said, looking at her phone. "Maybe it's like a stage name."

Spenser knew that humans sometimes used a name they were not given as a way to hide their identity. He and his brothers had all taken names from the human movies and shows they'd watched before coming to Earth. There was nothing wrong with choosing a new name, as far as he knew.

Unless you were using it to hide something.

"May I see the map?" Natalie asked.

Vi handed her a page.

The topography didn't stand out to her right away, but the colors did.

On the page were three color-coded lines, a red, a blue and a green. The red and blue were fairly close, running parallel to each other. The green line was much further east.

"This looks like a roadway plan," Natalie said, squinting some writing along the edge. "Look, it's a little out of focus, but I think it says PennDot in the lower right corner here."

"A roadway plan?" Jana echoed.

"I've seen plans like this before, when they were putting in the roundabout near town center," Natalie explained. "They always give optional routes, in case one doesn't work out. That's why there are three lines in alternate colors.

There's a URL here, too. It must be the engineering firm that drew them up."

Natalie slid her phone out of her pocket and typed in the web address. She could feel the others holding their breath.

In a few seconds, a stock photo image of a smiling man in a hardhat greeted her. She clicked on the menu for *About Us* and read the mission statement.

"It looks like they specialize in highway design and planning," she said, looking up at her friends.

"Let me see that map again," Vi said, grabbing it. "Yeah, that's definitely Stargazer. There's the orchard, there's the pond. It even has the new roundabout."

"So they're bringing in a highway," Natalie breathed.

"What does this mean?" Spenser asked.

Vi looked up from the map, her eyes blazing. "It means my sister is a very greedy woman."

"The attention this town is getting because of aliens means we're a destination now," Jana said. "I guess a highway would help relieve congestion on the local roads leading here, and encourage more tourism too."

"And if a highway is approved, the government will buy up the land for it," Natalie said. "They'll pay the local market price per square foot, even though this land is worth far less than typical market value."

"The agreements back that up," Vi said, nodding.

"So whoever just bought the land can sell it at a profit to the government when they build the highway?" Jana asked.

"Bingo," Vi said.

"But the mayor wanted that area for the MacroFoods executive housing campus," Natalie said. "He had already negotiated a right-of-first refusal with a farmer out that way. He told me all about it. Several times."

She remembered Saturday mornings, sitting in his

office, drinking coffee together as he enthused about one plan or another while he worked on the weekly anagram puzzle in the local paper. She felt her throat hitch at the thought that she would never get to enjoy time with him like that again.

"Where's the farm?" Vi asked, handing her the map and snapping her back to the present.

Natalie studied it, eager to keep her mind occupied on the task at hand. There would be time for grief when this was all over.

"Here," she said, pointing at the farm in question.

It was at the exact center of the map. The red and blue lines both went through it.

"My God," Natalie breathed.

"Natalie," Spenser said worriedly. "Are you okay?'

"What is it?" Jana demanded.

"I'll have to piece together the plot maps and deeds like a puzzle to be sure," Vi said. "But I think it's going to turn out that the people behind Kendra Z. Bose corp. hedged their bets by purchasing land along the red and blue routes, but not the green."

"So if Mayor Smalls ruined their shot at getting the last parcel in the way of those routes, they would be out a ton of money, with nothing to show for it but a whole lot of worthless land," Vi said. "The government wouldn't pull eminent domain on a brand-new housing complex if they could just go with the green route instead."

She stopped, looking like she didn't want to say the next part.

"With that much money on the line, the corporation might have been willing to do anything to stop the mayor from completing his deal," Natalie said quietly, since Vi wouldn't say it. "Including murder him."

A hush fell on their group.

Natalie looked over at Vi, who wore an expression of consternation.

"I don't get along with my sister," Vi said. "But something about this doesn't add up."

"She's just the attorney," Jana pointed out.

But Vi shook her head. "She didn't keep electronic records of these transactions. She knew this was fishy. And I suspect Myra is involved financially based on one of these spreadsheets."

"Why?" Hannibal asked.

"Look at all those contributions ending in 12," Vi said, pointing to the spreadsheet in question. "She never passes up a chance to slip her lucky number into a business venture."

"I'm so sorry, Vi," Natalie said quietly.

"Don't be sorry yet," Vi said. "Myra's a total asshole. But I don't think she was involved in a murder."

Natalie opened her mouth and closed it again.

She had seen this exact scene play out a thousand times in her line of work.

No one ever wanted to believe that their sibling, their neighbor, their colleague or spin instructor was capable of committing a crime, especially a serious one.

If someone close to you could do something like that, it meant you had to acknowledge that you were capable too, or that anyone was.

And that idea was scary enough that no one wanted to face it. It was so much easier to say *she would never...*

"I just need some time to figure it out," Vi said, looking up at Natalie pleadingly.

Natalie fought her better judgment, acutely aware of all

the eyes in the room on her, waiting. She could let this go. She wasn't even supposed to be investigating.

But then what would that make her?

"I will give you twenty-four hours," she heard herself say. "After that, I'll have to do the right thing."

She got up quickly and headed out of the room.

She knew she was the bad guy now, the suspended cop who was going to turn in Vi's sister.

But there was a right way, and there was a wrong way. And she was already bending the rules to the breaking point.

She jogged down the stairs to get Barker Posey and her leash.

Hopefully, a good walk would clear her mind.

And maybe she could look into finding someplace new to live. If the others were as loyal to Vi as she suspected, Natalie was going to need a new place sooner rather than later.

15

SPENSER

Spenser watched Natalie go.

He wavered between following her and letting her be.

"Give her a little space," Jana suggested quietly.

"I'm going to think," Vi said, heading back toward her room.

"She's going to play that game," Jana said with an alarmed look on her face.

When Vi needed to think, she played a game of her own invention, *Dancypants 2*, which involved a set of sensors on her pants, an amplifier, and some very loud dance music.

"Come downstairs with us," Fletcher suggested.

Jana looked between the brothers and shook her head.

"I'll do you one better," she offered. "I'll go get us all some comfort food. See you guys in twenty minutes."

"Thank you," Fletcher said, smiling at her so tenderly that Spenser had to look away.

She kissed him on top of his head and headed out.

"Let's go down to our place," Hannibal said.

Spenser allowed himself to hope that Natalie and Barker

Posey would be there waiting for him. But it was probably a good idea either way.

They headed into the hallway and down to the second-floor landing. But when Hannibal opened the door to their apartment, there was no one home to greet them.

Spenser fought to hide his emotions.

"She'll be back, brother," Fletcher said, throwing an arm over his shoulder.

"I don't know," Spenser said.

It was too hard to articulate the hint of iciness he had seen in Natalie's expression when she turned away from them, the slight exaggeration in her normally excellent posture as she walked out the door.

These things were infinitesimal, but to him they communicated volumes.

A wall had gone up between Spenser and his mate. And he had no idea how to tear it down.

Or if she even wanted him to.

"We could tell something was different between the two of you this morning," Hannibal said. "Did she accept you?"

"No," Spenser shook his head sadly, wishing he could bring himself to regret restraining himself. Her desire had been so intense last night that she would have accepted him just to soothe her body. He didn't want that to be the reason she accepted him. "But we talked about it. And I think she would have been ready to accept me soon."

Not soon. Tonight.

He had hoped she would accept him tonight. And he hadn't been sure how he would even wait that long.

Now the future stretched out before him endlessly. A parched desert and Natalie was his only hope of rain.

"She is your mate, brother," Fletcher said. "She will accept you. You must give her space."

"Space for what?" he demanded, losing his temper. "Space to forget me, to find someone else? Space to decide she doesn't need to bind herself to an alien?"

He managed not to say *bind herself to an alien and his whole extended family.* He knew by instinct that her conflict with Vi was at least part of reason for leaving.

But some things should not be said.

And he could not find it in himself to truly resent his brother, or his brother's mate.

They were good people, and they were all just doing their best.

A few minutes later, the door opened and Jana came in, carrying with her the heavenly scent of cheeseburgers and French fries.

"There wasn't even a line," she said happily, laying out her purchases on the coffee table.

Hannibal put a milkshake in Spenser's hand and Spenser took a long pull.

The cold, creamy chocolate filled his senses and he truly did feel a moment of relief from his pain.

"Everything will be alright, brother," Hannibal said, thumping him on the back and handing him a cheeseburger. "Just wait and see."

"Is this about Natalie?" Jana asked with sparkling eyes. "*Man* does she have the hots for you, Spenser."

Spenser grinned, delighted at this observation.

Maybe his brothers were right, and things would be just fine.

Somehow.

16

NATALIE

Natalie loaded Barker Posey into her car, followed by her backpack, and then herself.

Her whole world seemed to be falling down around her ears, but at least she traveled light.

She pulled out onto Crescent and headed for the main drag out of Stargazer, not even knowing why she was going that way.

"What am I doing?" she asked Barker Posey.

The big dog just grinned at her and drooled a little.

Natalie smiled back and felt a little better.

In times of personal struggle, she was used to turning to work to soothe her mind. But now she couldn't even do that.

Or could she?

She pulled over and slid out her phone again, glad she had snapshots of all the documents.

One of the sales agreements had an addendum allowing the owner to occupy the property for a little longer. The name on that one had looked familiar.

"Gretchen Ramirez," she read out loud.

Natalie had gone to school with a Jodi Ramirez who lived out that way.

She put her phone away and pulled her car out again. The Ramirez place was only a few miles away. She turned up the radio, enjoying the distraction of the short road trip as much as possible.

A few minutes later, she and Barker Posey got out in front of a small cottage at the end of a long private drive.

The door opened as they approached.

"I hope I didn't startle you," a woman said. "I heard the car coming down the drive, and I don't get many surprise guests."

"Good evening, ma'am," Natalie said. "I was hoping you might be willing to answer a few questions."

"You're that West girl, aren't you?" the woman asked. "You're a cop now. Am I in some sort of trouble?"

"No, not at all," Natalie said, trying to use the friendliest tone she could muster. "And yes, I'm the West girl. Your daughter is Jodi, right?"

"That she is," the woman said. "I'm Gretchen. Won't you come in?"

"We can talk out here," Natalie said. "I don't want to impose, especially with the dog."

She glanced down at Barker Posey, who was sitting politely and smiling at Gretchen Ramirez.

"Oh nonsense," Gretchen said, smiling back. "He's a love. Come on in."

Natalie followed her into the house, not bothering to correct the dog's gender.

The house was small but tidy. A stack of boxes lined one wall.

"Can I fix you some coffee?" Gretchen asked. "I don't have much more. I'm getting ready to move."

"Oh, I'm fine," Natalie said. "Where are you headed?"

"I'm going to stay with my sister-in-law for a little while," Gretchen replied. "After that, I'm not sure. Since Paco died, I've been kind of spinning my wheels."

"I'm so sorry for your loss," Natalie said, meaning it.

"Thank you," Gretchen said. "Anyway, when that lawyer lady came to say they wanted my land, I figured it was a sign to move on."

"Do you know who she represented?" Natalie asked.

"Nah," Gretchen said. "It's just some company. I didn't pay too much attention when I saw they were offering a fair price as-is. I figured she was on the up and up, since she had the chief of police with her."

A cold chill went down Natalie's spine.

"What did you just say?" she asked.

"Chief Baker was with her every time she came here," Gretchen repeated. "Is that normal?"

Natalie shook her head, her mind spinning.

"Well, I'll tell you what, they paid up fast and even let me stay an extra month to pack," Gretchen confided. "So as far as I'm concerned, she could have brought the Queen of England if she wanted."

Natalie nodded.

The truth was beginning to come together in her mind. She thought about the chief refusing to let her investigate the mayor's death.

She thought about the mayor, sitting at his desk with a word puzzle, and her mind latched on to something about the name of the corporation on those documents.

It couldn't be that simple.

Could it?

"You sure you don't want some coffee?" Gretchen asked. "You look like you just saw a ghost."

She needed to go.

"I'm fine, really," Natalie said. "Thank you so much for talking with me. This has been so helpful."

"If you say so," Gretchen said dubiously.

Natalie managed to get herself and Barker Posey back to the car. Before she pulled out her notepad and wrote down the name of the mystery company in block letters at the top of the page.

KENDRA Z. BOSE.

She crossed them off one at a time as she rearranged them into a new name in the space below. When she was through, she sighed and looked at her handiwork.

BAKERS DOZEN.

Apparently, Mayor Smalls hadn't been the only one who liked anagrams. He probably never guessed his hobby wold help solve his own murder.

Natalie studied the notepad.

BAKERS DOZEN.

It wasn't exactly proof, but it was too perfect to be a coincidence. It had the chief's name in it, plain as day. Plus the number twelve reference that Myra liked to sneak in.

Natalie had a strong feeling that she would find all the proof she needed with a close look at Myra Croft's and Chief Baker's finances.

How had they missed that?

And what was she supposed to do with this new piece of intel? Her instincts urged her to share it with Vi and the others, but she suspected she was the last person any of them wanted to see right now.

No. It was better for her to finish this on her own. No matter how much she wanted to lose herself in Spenser's warm embrace and forget about the rest of the world for a while.

Barker Posey gave her a firm lick on the ear and whined, bringing her back to the present.

The poor thing was probably hungry.

And she had forgotten the bag of dog food back at 221 B Crescent Street.

"We'll just run back and grab it, then see if we can find a good AirBnB," Natalie told the dog.

But it was more of a promise to herself.

She couldn't afford any more distractions.

17

NATALIE

Natalie knocked on the apartment door.

She had only spent one night in this house, but it was odd to knock, the place already felt strangely familiar to her.

Spenser opened the door, looked down at her, and smiled as if he had just won the lottery.

"You came home," he said in a deep, gruff voice.

Home...

Be strong, Natalie.

"I forgot the dog's stuff," she said, not making eye contact.

"Oh," he said, stepping back immediately. "Sure, I'll help you."

She could feel his pain as if it were her own, like a knife between her ribs.

He was already heading into the kitchen.

She trailed behind him like a ghost.

"I will help you leave if that's what you want," he told her, bending to pick up Barker Posey's water dish and heading to the sink with it. "But I hope you'll reconsider."

"This whole situation is so sticky," Natalie said, grateful that he had his back to her, so she could speak without having to look at his face. "It doesn't feel right to be staying here in Vi's space with her family, when I know what I'm going to have to do."

"You don't know yet, right?" Spenser asked, turning to her. "Vi still has overnight to look into it."

"Yes," Natalie agreed. "That's what I promised her, and I'm a woman of my word. But I should never have made that promise."

"Why not?" Spenser asked.

"Because that's not how it's done," Natalie said. "Waiting gives the suspect time to cover their tracks. Every minute is valuable in law enforcement."

"You think Vi will warn her sister," Spenser realized out loud.

He wasn't wrong.

"Not necessarily," Natalie hedged. "Myra's smart. She could notice that someone has been in her files. The assistant will tell her the door was open."

"Hm," Spenser said.

She felt a tug in the bond between them.

Being mates means we are honest with each other, no matter what...

"I also worry that Vi will tell Myra," Natalie admitted. "Not because Vi is a bad person, but because family is family."

"Loyalty is hard to shake," Spenser said, nodding. "And Vi is a loyal person. But I believe she sees Hannibal and Jana as her family even more than Myra."

That was very possibly true, and the main reason Natalie had given her time.

But a good cop wouldn't have done it.

She had allowed her emotions to interfere.

And she couldn't allow that to happen again.

"Well, I guess we should get going," Natalie said, nodding down at Barker Posey, who was half asleep on the end of her leash.

"Why don't you stay here for the night?" Spenser offered. "You can have my room. I'll sleep in Hannibal's since he'll be downstairs. You can wrap things up here in the morning if you need to, and find another place if you think it's best. But, Natalie... I hope you will stay."

Her heart twisted and writhed in her chest, but she took a deep breath and steeled herself. It wasn't fair to him to keep him dangling like this.

"Spenser, I'm attracted to you and I care about you a lot," she began. "But I don't like the way I've changed since we got involved. It's important to me to do the right thing. But from the moment we laid eyes on each other I've been sneaking around, breaking and entering, bending the rules... It doesn't feel like me. I need to go back to my regular life. I know you'll find another mate, someone cut out for the life you have here with your brothers."

His face had fallen steadily as she spoke. She watched him for a moment, hoping he wouldn't fight her on this. She wasn't sure she could hold up to an argument with this man who made her heart pound so fast.

"I understand, Natalie," he said. "I would never want you to be unhappy. But there will never be another mate for me. If you ever change your mind, I will be here, waiting for you."

She nodded, not trusting herself to speak.

"I still hope you will stay here for the night," he went on. "It's too late to look for another place. You have my promise that I won't come near you. I just want to know you and Barker Posey are okay."

"Thank you," she whispered.

It was impossible not to notice that in a world where her mentor was dead, the chief was involved in a shady land deal, a prominent local attorney was likely a murderer, and even Natalie herself was behaving out of character, Spenser was still himself - true to his core.

It was going to be hell letting go of him.

But what choice did she have?

18

SPENSER

Spenser lay in bed, gazing out the window at the moonlight filtering through the trees.

It was odd to be borrowing his brother's room, sleeping in a different bed.

But it was even more odd to know that Natalie was just on the other side of the wall, sleeping in his bed again, this time without him.

His heart ached at the memory of her words.

I don't like the way I've changed since we got involved...

He loved and supported her the best way he knew how. But what she had said told him he'd gotten everything wrong.

As her mate, it was his job to help her feel confident.

And deeper than that, it was his job to help her be her best self.

The trouble was, when Spenser looked at Natalie, he didn't see that she needed fixing.

She was brave and smart and always ready to lend a hand. If there was some better version of her, he could not imagine it.

He didn't think she'd made a mistake. In fact, her compassion toward Vi had only made him love her more.

Natalie was an excellent detective. Even if Myra was truly guilty, and if allowing extra time gave her more time to weave her web, he was still very sure that Natalie would prevail.

And she would do it with a clear conscience, knowing she had not betrayed a friend.

That was what Vi was to her now, a friend. Though they had seen each other as rivals from the beginning, Spenser could see the friendship between them growing, a palpable thing, born of their shared need to find the truth at all costs.

Natalie might not see it now, but Spenser suspected she would be sleeping even less soundly if she had gone after Myra without allowing Vi a shot at cracking the case.

Unfortunately, it was not his privilege to point these things out to Natalie. She was not yet his mate and she had not asked for his opinion.

But he felt as if he were watching his whole existence collapse, knowing she was in pain and unable to help her.

Surely there was something he could do.

He closed his eyes and called up an image of her. Natalie always stood tall and proud. Unlike himself and his brothers, she didn't glance at anyone else for confirmation before taking action.

Natalie was independent.

No.

Natalie was alone. She had always been alone. She had told him so.

I don't have any siblings. We moved a lot when I was a kid, so I didn't have a lot of friends. I've always been self-reliant.

But she didn't have to be.

She had friends now. She had Spenser. She had Vi and the others. She had Barker Posey.

If Natalie wanted, she could be the un-loneliest woman in Stargazer.

All he had to do was tell her.

No.

He had to show her.

Spenser was used to being part of a team, giving help but also taking it when he needed it.

Natalie didn't know what it was like to have someone who would always have her back one hundred percent of the time.

It was his job to find a way to show her.

He placed his palm against the wall that separated him from her and tried to feel beyond the cool drywall to the warm woman on the other side.

I'm coming, Natalie. I'm going to have your back tomorrow. No matter what.

19

NATALIE

The next morning Natalie stood by her car in front of 221B with Barker Posey on the end of her leash, waiting patiently while she talked on the phone.

"You know you could both be risking your badges over this, right?" Natalie asked.

"You've got good intel," Lance said. "If the chief is involved in this, we don't have a choice. It's the right thing to do."

"Besides, he can't fire all three of us," Lila pointed out. "The force isn't that big. And isn't that what we have a union for?"

They were both being brave.

Natalie's evidence was shaky at best, and not even the union could save them if her hunch was wrong.

The truth was, these two colleagues on the phone trusted her.

Please God, let me be right about this. They're good people and I can't let them down.

"Thank you both," she said, her voice a little husky.

"Don't get sappy on us, West," Lance teased. "At least, not yet. Let's go get your perp first."

She hung up and turned to look up at Spenser's window.

Instead, she got a fantastic view of the man himself as he stepped out the front door.

"I didn't mean to eavesdrop," he said, looking a little embarrassed. "But I couldn't risk you leaving without me."

"What are you talking about?" Natalie asked.

"I'm here to help you," he told her. "I have your back, always."

"Even when my intention is to arrest your new sister-in-law's sister?" she asked.

"Especially then," he said solemnly. "Anyone can do the right thing on their own when it's easy."

"Thank you," she told him, feeling a sense of relief that went further than just having someone to ride shotgun on a big day. "Let's go, then."

Barker Posey hopped into her regular spot in the back as Natalie and Spenser got in the front.

"I don't know what's going to happen," she warned him.

"You've got this," he told her contentedly. "And you've got me, just in case things get ugly."

They drove on in silence for a few minutes. It was almost calming, but they arrived at the law firm far too quickly.

She took a steadying breath and got out with Barker Posey.

Spenser followed them to the door, where Lance and Lila were already waiting.

"Ready?" Natalie asked.

"You know it," Lance said, looking less confident than he sounded.

"Absolutely," Lila added, nodding.

"No matter what," Spenser told her.

Something about his deep voice sent her heart into a double backflip. She wasn't used to relying on anyone else, but it was nice to know someone had her back.

It was a feeling she could see herself getting used to.

She pushed the door open before she could overthink it.

"Not *you* again," the assistant said in an exasperated way. "*Myra.*"

Spenser and the two officers filed in behind her as Myra stepped out of her office, and Barker Posey suddenly began to bark with the force of an explosion.

Natalie almost dropped the leash she was so shocked. She had never heard the big dog bark at anyone before.

Myra moved to Kendall's desk as if to shield herself. To his credit, her assistant stood his ground, putting himself between her and the potential danger.

"Stop that thing at once," she insisted.

Barker Posey's hackles rose, and she went to the end of her leash, barking like crazy, as if she wanted to attack.

It was so unlike her, that Natalie didn't quite know how to react. But it occurred to her that the big dog had probably been pretty traumatized by watching her master die. It was no wonder she wasn't acting like herself.

And if Myra had been there, had been responsible…

Was Barker Posey trying to tell her something?

The door behind Natalie flew open.

She turned to see Vi, followed by the others.

"I gave you your shot," Natalie warned.

"Yes, you did, and I'm grateful for that," Vi said. "Will you trust me one more time?"

"What do you want?" Natalie asked, trying to restrain the dog, who was struggling so hard she was threatening to break the leash.

"Let the dog off the leash," Vi said simply.

"Seriously?" Natalie asked, glancing at the furious dog.

"Yes," Vi said. "Let her off the leash."

Natalie glanced over at Spenser.

He nodded, looking gratified.

For a moment Natalie wavered. If the dog hurt Myra, she could be held responsible. Or it might cause enough of a commotion for her to get away.

But...

She looked around the room at all the people who had shown up for her, trusting her, with or without proof.

And Spenser was here. Showing up for her, backing her up even after she made it clear that she had no intention of accepting him as her mate.

She tried to bring up a picture of the mayor in her mind, to remind herself why she had to do this on her own.

Instead, she saw him as he was during one of the last times she'd seen him, feeding logs into the fire in his shadowy study, smiling up at her with those crinkly eyes.

Open your heart, Nat, he had told her that night. *I can't be the most important guy in your life forever.*

Natalie West opened her eyes and decided to trust her friends.

She unclipped Barker Posey's leash.

Everything else seemed to happen in slow motion.

The dog rushed the desk, completely ignoring Myra, but nearly knocking the assistant over.

Myra screamed and Barker Posey appeared on the other side of the desk again, carrying something in her mouth.

"My bag," the assistant yelled.

Barker Posey dropped the leather satchel in front of Natalie and nosed at it frantically.

"What is it, girl?" Natalie asked her.

The big dog whined and looked up at her with tragic eyes.

"Y-you don't have a warrant," the assistant said. "You can't search that."

"No, but she can," Natalie said, allowing the big dog to keep trying. "She's a private citizen. Unless you'd like to try to stop her?"

The assistant's face turned very pale.

Out of the corner of her eye, Natalie could see that Vi had out her phone and was recording the whole scene.

The dog somehow managed to overturn the satchel at last. She pounced on a particular item and held it out to Natalie gingerly in her teeth.

The air went out of Natalie's lungs.

"Natalie, what is it?" Spenser's voice was low and calm.

"It's his EpiPen," Natalie said, her voice sounded like paper, dry and thin. "It's the mayor's."

"No, it's mine," Kendall said quickly. "I'm allergic to bees."

"It's not yours," Natalie said quietly.

The pen had a label on it with the mayor's prescription info. The words *Study- desk drawer* were jotted on the label too, in the mayor's wobbly cursive.

Natalie felt her legs go out from under her and she sat down on the floor.

Barker Posey began nosing her.

"Good girl," Natalie told her. "You did just right. You knew just what he needed, and who had it. I'm sorry we're too late. I'm so sorry."

The big dog didn't seem to mind Natalie's tears wetting her silky fur.

"Kendall, what the hell is going on?" Myra demanded.

"You were in so much trouble," Kendall said quietly, in a defeated voice. "You were in over your head."

"I'm never in over my head," Myra retorted automatically.

"You invested all your money. You invested some of the clients' escrows," Kendall said. "You even put your sister's trust fund money into that project."

There was a hush in the room.

This time Myra didn't interrupt.

"And he was going to ruin it," Kendall went on. "He was going to ruin *you*."

"So you *killed him*?" Myra demanded.

"No, I would never do that," Kendall said, looking defeated. "I just went there to talk to him. I hoped I could convince him to do the right thing. With you and the Chief Baker involved, I thought maybe I could get through to him."

Natalie pictured it, Kendall taking the company car out to see the mayor that night. No wonder the car spotted leaving the scene was licensed to Myra.

"He was really nice," Kendall said. "He let me in without an appointment. He even offered me a lemon bar."

That tracked. The mayor liked to see young people take initiative.

"But I couldn't convince him to let the housing idea go," Kendall went on. "He listened, but he told me he disagreed. And that he thought Myra was bright and hardworking and that she would find another way to make a fortune. I didn't want to tell him about the things you were doing," he said, turning to Myra. "You know, the stuff with other people's money."

Myra glared at him like she wanted to set him on fire.

"Anyway, I was desperate. I was about to start crying,"

Kendall said. "Then he took a lemon square for himself. I think he was trying to give me a minute to pull myself together. He didn't want me to know that he'd seen I was about to cry."

That was the mayor all over. Natalie had seen him do almost anything to let another person save face. It was one of the reasons so many people loved him, and why he was so good at what he did.

"Then all of a sudden his face was swelling up, and he was gagging and choking," Kendall said. "He reached into his desk and he pulled out the EpiPen. But it slipped out of his hands and rolled under the desk."

Natalie waited, knowing what was coming next, but not wanting to hear it.

"I don't know what came over me," Kendall said. "But it landed right at my feet. So... I just... grabbed it. And I shoved it in my bag, and then I ran out and drove away."

"You *killed* him," Myra screamed.

"I didn't think he would actually die," Kendall said. "I just wanted to hurt him for what he was doing to you."

"Why would you do that?" Myra yelled. "Why would you ever do something so stupid? It was only money. I could have paid it back. I could have earned more."

Natalie stared at Myra, wondering how she could see something so clearly that Myra obviously couldn't see at all.

"Because he loves you, Myra," Vi said suddenly.

Myra stared at him, speechless.

"She's right," Kendall whispered miserably.

Myra looked back at her sister, eyes like fiery daggers.

"You don't know the first thing about love," Myra spat. "You're like a robot. All you care about is solving puzzles."

"You're wrong," Vi said calmly. "I know all about love. And I hope one day you'll get to know about it too."

"But first she's going to spend some time behind bars," Lila said. "And so is Romeo here. Lance, read them their rights."

"Come on, guys," Jana said, waving them to the door. "Let's get some fresh air."

"Don't go anywhere," Lance warned them. "We'll need to take statements."

"Of course not," Jana said. "We just want to give you space."

Spenser reached down to where Natalie still sat on the floor with the dog, offering her his hands, pulling her up and into his arms for a hug that warmed her body and soul.

This had been a horrible, ugly morning.

But it was better to know the truth.

Natalie West was going to be okay.

She was going to be better than okay. She was going to be part of a team.

20

SPENSER

A few hours later, Spenser sat on the sofa in Vi and Jana's apartment on the top floor of 221B.

His arm was around Natalie, and she was leaning against him, relaxed.

After all the questioning, the reports, and the paperwork, they had finally been sent home.

Jana had ordered a massive delivery of Thai food on the drive back and the six friends had just finished gorging themselves.

Even Barker Posey was gnawing half-heartedly on the bone from a T-bone steak Vi had pulled out of the freezer for her.

"So do you think you'll be up for the chief's job?" Vi asked Natalie. "I'm assuming his involvement in this mess will be the end of his career."

"You're probably right about that," Natalie said, shaking her head. "But I don't think that's a job for me."

"Why not?" Vi asked. "You've been with the Stargazer force for a while, and you blew this case wide open, in spite of the odds being stacked against you."

"I think I've spent enough time on the force," Natalie said. "I'm going to apply for a job in the private sector."

"I thought being a police officer was your dream," Spenser said worriedly. He didn't want her to stop doing what she had always wanted to do.

"I've had a chance to really think today," Natalie said slowly. "What I've always wanted was to seek out the truth. Being a cop was one means to that end. But it's not the only way."

Suddenly, Vi had a knowing smile on her face. She gave Natalie an imperceptible nod.

"What's going on?" Spenser asked. He didn't always follow the subtle cues of human conversations in real life. In the movies, everyone always said exactly what they were thinking. It was much easier that way.

"What's going on is that I'm asking Vi for a job," Natalie said. "I know it's a new organization. I'm willing to work for a cut of the cases I solve. You don't have to answer me now, Vi, but—"

"You're hired," Vi said.

Natalie grinned at her and Vi grinned back.

"Holy cow," Jana said.

"You can't actually be surprised, Jana," Vi said. "Natalie and I work really well together. We have complementary strengths. Plus there's the family connection."

"What family connection?" Jana asked.

"She's Spenser's bonded mate," Vi said. "Which means sooner or later the six of us will be related. You too, Barker Posey. I guess you'll be my niece."

Barker Posey looked up from her bone for a minute, panted in a friendly way, and then went back to work.

"You're Spenser's bonded mate?" Jana asked Natalie.

"I'm about to be," Natalie said. "If he still wants me."

She glanced up at him.

He could tell from the playful twinkle in her eyes that she was teasing. She knew how desperately he wanted her. She could never doubt it.

"We have to go now," Spenser announced, lifting her up and heading for the door.

"What?" Vi asked. "Where are you going?"

"I'm claiming my mate," Spenser announced as Natalie melted into giggles in his arms. "We'll be downstairs. Don't join us unless you want to watch."

"Is that an option?" Fletcher asked.

Hannibal smacked his head.

Fletcher let his head drop back and howled like a hyena.

But Spenser missed whatever happened next. He was carrying Natalie onto the landing and down the stairs to his apartment.

She was still giggling, but she was also nuzzling her face into his neck, driving him wild with her tickle of warm breath.

"If there's any chance you're going to change your mind, you need to tell me now," he growled as he flung open the door to the apartment.

"Not a chance," she whispered in his ear. "I want you. Forever."

A pang of need shot through him and he nearly forgot how to walk.

She nuzzled in closer and he managed to stride down the hallway and kick open the door of his room.

"Spenser," she murmured.

He placed her down gently. "Natalie, I want you so much," he told her. "Are you ready to accept me?"

"Yes, please," she whispered back, tearing at her own clothing in obvious frustration.

"Wait, let me help you," he murmured, finding some shred of his own patience, now that she had lost hers.

He tried his best to take his time removing their garments, tenderly kissing her sweet flesh as he exposed it, bit by bit.

He knew that when it was done, he would take her swiftly, whether he meant to or not. He had resisted for too long already.

At last, they were both bare in the moonlight of his small room.

"It was so lonely in here without you last night," she told him. "I wanted you so much that it hurt."

"I slept with my hand against the wall so I could be as close as possible," he admitted. "Neither of us will ever suffer such loneliness again."

She went up on her toes, pressing her lips to his, sending his head into the stars.

Her body felt so good, warm, and bare against him, her soft curves pressed to his chiseled muscle.

He kissed her for as long as he could bear it, then guided her to the bed and gently lowered her down.

She reached her arms out for him.

He shook his head and nudged her thighs apart.

She allowed him the access he craved, and his body sang with the glory of it.

He lowered his face to taste her.

She moaned at the touch of his tongue, tossing her head against the pillow.

He closed his eyes, savoring her every sound and movement, and prayed for the strength to please her properly before his own needs overwhelmed him.

21

NATALIE

Natalie closed her eyes against the onslaught of sensations.

There was the acute physical need Spenser was stoking in her with each lash of his clever tongue. But there was also an emptiness in her heart that hungered for him on a deeper level.

"I need you," she murmured, when he had pushed her body and soul to their quivering limits.

Instantly, he stopped and crawled up to her, caging her head in his arms and gazing down at her with such intensity that she thought her heart would forget to beat.

"I am yours, and you are mine," he told her, pressing his forehead to hers.

"Yes, yes," she murmured back, her hips lifting to meet his, her whole essence attuned to him, ready to accept him in every way possible.

When he entered her at last, she had to close her eyes against the pleasure of it.

"Look at me," he said with a low growl that was impossible to ignore.

She opened her eyes again and he locked his gaze on her.

Everything in her tightened, the pleasure, the love she felt for this man whose loyalty had opened her heart.

"Spenser," she whispered as he filled her again and again until she was consumed with need.

When the pleasure finally took her, it felt like a hurricane rushing through her blood and ravaging her body.

Spenser shouted her name and she felt him fall apart with her, both of them greedy for every wave and every tremor of the other's ecstasy.

For a long time afterward, he held her in his arms, stroking her back.

"My mate," he whispered. "Rest now, sweet one."

It was early, and she had more to do.

But it had been such a long day already.

And they had all the time in the world together.

She felt herself drifting into sleep, knowing that this was only the beginning.

22

SPENSER

Spenser stood on the moonlit beach beside his brothers.

They were all dressed in suits, and looking very much like movie stars, in his opinion.

They were also very nervous.

"Everything's fine, boys, really," Micah reassured them. "Tony is the most organized man in the world, and the ceremony is simple. You're going to be fine."

"Thank you, Micah," Hannibal said with feeling.

"It's my pleasure," Micah replied, clapping him on the shoulder. "I love weddings. Of course Tony and I threw a bigger shindig than this, but that's our style. I think you and the girls chose just right."

Spenser looked around at the natural beauty of this place. The deep blue of the night sky seemed to melt into the sparkling depths of the ocean. The moon reflected in its frothy surface, bobbing like a glowing ball.

Footprints through the cream-colored sand led back to the little house where the women were getting ready.

Soon, Natalie would be here, and he would be her husband.

The mating bond they already shared was permanent, and from what he understood, human marriage was not.

But he wanted to honor her traditions and be bound with her in any way that might be meaningful to her people.

Tony began to play the acoustic guitar from where he sat on a bright blue beach chair.

A small group of friends and family sat in a half-circle around him, facing the water. Torches danced around them, adding their brightness to the pale moonlit sand.

From the cottage, a small figure appeared, carrying a bouquet of flowers.

It was Vi, she was smiling in a half-embarrassed way, walking a little too quickly over the sandy drifts to get to Hannibal. A short, ivory gown just skimmed her calves and made her look taller than usual.

Beside him, Hannibal stood up a little straighter.

When Vi passed through the half-circle of torches to reach them, her expression softened.

The love she felt for Hannibal was a palpable thing, strong and sure.

Spenser smiled as he watched them take each other's hands.

But Fletcher wasn't watching.

Spenser followed his line of sight to see that Jana had nearly reached the torches, and his brother's gaze was locked on her every step.

She stood tall and proud, swathed in white satin in a way that made her look like one of the Greek statues at the art museum - even more than usual. She walked smoothly toward Fletcher, who beheld her with a look of wonder on his face.

Spenser watched until she entered the circle.

Then he looked up, anticipation heating his blood.

Natalie was already walking toward him across the sand.

Her dark hair was twisted up into a bun on her head, revealing the elegant curve of her neck. She wore a simple white dress that clung to her hips and breasts. Moonlight glowed in the light fabric as if it were as enchanted with her as Spenser was.

He gazed at her, rapt and breathless at her beauty.

Her walk to him seemed to take forever. He tried to memorize each movement, and the way she looked back at him, so solemn and yet so joyful.

At last, she crossed the torch line to join him.

Her hands were soft in his, and they turned as one to the new mayor of Stargazer, who spoke the words of the ceremony to each couple in turn.

Before long, it was Spenser and Natalie's turn to make their promises.

He did his best to repeat the words, but he was so hypnotized by her smile that he hardly knew what he was saying. In the end, he was allowed to slip the slender band of gold around her finger and kiss her.

The tiny crowd cheered, and Tony even whistled as Spenser dipped Natalie low and kissed her like their lives depended on it.

When he finally set her on her feet again, she laughed and nuzzled his neck.

"Now what?" he asked her.

"Well, I guess there's going to be food and dancing," she told him.

"Not too much food and dancing," he growled. "I want to get you back to our cottage."

She smiled and cupped his jaw in her little hand. "You'll never be satisfied," she teased.

"Never," he agreed, tilting his head to kiss her palm.

He turned her around in his arms, and they watched the others greeting their friends, smiling and laughing.

It was a perfect night. Just like every night since Natalie had agreed to be his mate.

He glanced up at the stars, wondering at how quickly this planet had begun to feel like home.

"Are you thinking of Aerie?" Natalie asked quietly. "Are you homesick?"

"I am glad to be here with you," he answered her honestly. "Wherever you are is my home."

"Good," she told him with a smile. "Because I've already had jackets made up for the detective agency. It would be a shame to lose a member now. It's a wedding present for Vi."

"Should we give them to her now?" Spenser asked.

"Nah," Natalie said, watching Vi and Hannibal stealing a kiss just outside the circle of torchlight. "We've got time."

Spenser kissed the top of her head.

They did have time. They had forever. And he couldn't be happier about it.

***

Thanks for reading **Spenser**!

Did you know there are a whole BUNCH more books about these hunky Stargazer Aliens?

You can read all about that first wave of musclebound men from Aerie that started it all by making contact in the small town of Stargazer, Pennsylvania, or check out some of their brothers that followed in their footsteps in other locations. There is even a trilogy about the time someone decided to cash in on the alien craze with a reality TV show!

If that sounds good to you, then keep reading for sample of So You Think You Can Marry an Alien!

Or check out all the books in the Stargazer Series right here:

https://www.tashablack.com/stargazer.html

SO YOU THINK YOU CAN MARRY AN ALIEN - SAMPLE

1

MARGOT

Margot Lane glanced around the crowded room.
All around her, semi-famous and uber-wealthy people swayed to Elvis music in the dim light.

It was pretty cool, but it might have been cooler if they hadn't all been wearing plastic leis and grass skirts.

And trying not to think about food.

A couple of Kennedy cousins lounged on a velvet couch in the corner.

An auburn-haired woman - Margot swore she was one of the *Real Soccer Moms of the Gold Shore* - bent over the pool table, pretending to consider her best shot. She was really just flirting with her opponent, a starry-eyed personal trainer in a Hawaiian shirt.

It was Luau Day.

At this high-end secret fat camp for the one percent and their celebrity compatriots, there were a lot of themed days.

But in spite of the staff's efforts, every day felt pretty much the same at A Slender Start.

Margot's roommate, Saffy, sarcastically called the place

A Bulimic Beginning. The younger woman swore half the occupants were bribing the staff to smuggle in contraband candy.

Saffy had just finished her freshman year of college and her wealthy parents had sent her to A Slender Start to lose the freshman fifteen so she wouldn't embarrass them at the country club.

Margot felt very sorry for Saffy. She could hardly blame the girl for being sarcastic under the circumstances. Saffy had no real reason to be wasting her summer at fat camp.

Margot, on the other hand, had twenty-five good reasons.

"Can you believe this shit?" Saffy muttered, sidling up to Margot. "They don't even have a hula class. It's the exact same thing as the Fourth of July party, but with leis instead of flags. I'm going to get a drink."

"Hey, Saffy," Margot said, catching her hand before she got away.

"Yeah?"

"You're a really beautiful person," Margot told her.

"Um, thanks," Saffy said.

Even in the darkened room, Margot could practically hear her blush.

"I just wanted you to know that," Margot said. "You don't need to lose weight. You're perfect just the way you are."

"Are you angling for a low-sodium tomato juice of your very own?" Saffy asked. "Because I would have totally brought you one without all the ass-kissing."

Margot laughed and Saffy gave her a friendly shove and disappeared into the crowd, leaving Margot completely alone.

This was her chance.

She scanned the room for the trainers, but the only one in sight was about to take his turn at the pool table.

Before she could lose her nerve, Margot slipped between the bodies, making her way quickly, but smoothly toward the exit.

I'm an adult. I can just tell them I'm leaving and check out.

But she knew they would try to change her mind. Everyone would be watching.

And Margot Lane wasn't fond of confrontations.

Kind of ironic that she was there because most people saw her as the bloodthirsty and protective queen she played on TV.

Queen Esther of *A Lion's Game* would have dispatched with the bevy of trainers with a few cold words and a withering look.

She also would have been better at sneaking.

"Hey, Margot, how's it going?" Amberlee asked brightly as she appeared out of nowhere.

"Oh, hi, Amberlee," Margot muttered back to the petite trainer.

"Where are you headed?" Amberlee asked, a hint of suspicion creeping into her normally effervescent delivery.

"Just back to my room," Margot lied. "I forgot my lucky lei."

"Oh," Amberlee said, her blonde ponytail bouncing as she nodded. "Cool. Hurry back. You don't want to miss the hula."

"I don't think I could live with myself if I did," Margot said, nodding back.

Amberlee gave her a puzzled look and moved to rejoin the festivities as Margot made her way to the main lobby. No one was at the desk.

Perfect.

She passed the stairs and pushed through the big double doors that led outside. As soon as she hit daylight, she headed for the trees.

A Slender Start was a couple of miles from the nearest little town - Margot knew that much. But she figured she could sweep through the woods to get away from the camp, then come out at the main road, such as it was, and still make it back to the nearby village by dark.

Margot felt better the moment the green canopy of trees closed over her head. It was peaceful, with nothing but the hum of the cicadas and the squirrels scolding overhead.

She hiked uphill a little ways, enjoying the chance to fill her lungs with clean air and get some real exercise instead of the silly sit-ups she'd been doing with the trainers.

"Fit," Margot muttered to herself.

She'd spent a year tromping around the highlands of New Zealand in full armor wearing an auburn wig and a five-pound crown on top to shoot the first season of *A Lion's Game*. She was willing to bet she was more fit than most of her fans.

That hadn't mattered though. What mattered was what she looked like.

People want Queen Esther to look fit, like she is in the books.

And the producers had made her sweet agent tell her, a man who had six granddaughters.

"Oh, Margot, you know I'm proud of you, right?" Ed had asked, tears in his voice.

"Sure," she'd replied, figuring the show was canceled.

"They say the fans like your character, but…"

"But what?"

"You didn't test well overall near the end of the season. They think you're… too heavy," he'd said softly.

"Oh," she'd said, hurt but not surprised.

Margot exercised every day and ate well. She was a size ten, healthy and comfortable in her own skin. But show business seemed to reward the extremely slender, and no amount of dieting had ever gotten her much slimmer than she was now. She had been amazed and grateful to land the role as Queen Esther.

"They want to send you to a special summer retreat," Ed had continued. "To help you lose some weight. If you lose twenty-five pounds in the next four weeks, before shooting starts, you'll get to reprise your role."

"And if I don't?" she'd asked. "Are they really going to just replace me?"

"No," Ed had replied. "They're, uh, going to... kill off your character."

Margot had been unable to respond.

"You're a lovely young woman," Ed told her. "They say the camera adds ten pounds."

Then why don't they send the camera to fat camp?

But Margot never liked to cause a fuss.

So she had politely calmed Ed down and agreed that of course she would spend a month at A Slender Start and do her best to lose weight.

I'm a team player, she'd told herself. *It's for the good of the show. The whole cast is counting on me.*

But after a few days of abject boredom and condescension, she'd had enough. Anyone in her business who wasn't rail thin didn't need nutrition advice from a bunch of twenty-year old personal trainers. At this point, Margot knew so much about diet, exercise and metabolism that she could probably run her own fat camp.

But frankly she wasn't interested in running a fat camp, or attending one either.

Margot Lane was tired of being pushed around.

She wasn't sure what she did want to do, but whatever it was, it wasn't going to happen at A Slender Start in the next three weeks.

Now she just had to get out of the woods, make it to town, and plan her next move.

Without money or a cell phone.

Part of A Slender Start's impressive success ratio was that the place was run like a military camp. On arrival, they had taken Margot's phone and credit cards. She'd had to write an email to all her family and friends letting them know she was off the grid for a month and that they should not respond to her if she got in touch before the month was up - no matter what she said.

It wasn't a military camp. It was a cult.

And she wasn't sticking around to drink the Kool-Aid.

2

KENT

Kent tapped amiably on the top of the car and waved good-bye to his driver, Al.

Al grinned and waved back, looking a bit out of place in just his undershirt, with his hairy arms hanging out.

Kent was currently wearing Al's other shirt. He had borrowed it to disguise himself after he snuck out of the theater to visit his friend at the gas station.

The shirt was bright red with large white blossoms. Al had described it as a Hawaiian shirt. Kent recognized the style from the indomitable Magnum PI.

It was very lucky that the shirt fit both men. Al was short and round and Kent was tall and very muscular. This wasn't the first time they had done this, but each time Al removed an item of clothing he shook his head in wonder when Kent pulled it on.

"Thank you, Al," Kent called to him.

But Al was already looking at his mobile phone. Al had a girlfriend he liked to communicate with by typing words and symbols into the phone's screen.

Kent wasn't sure why they spoke that way when Al could easily turn the phone into a camera and see his girlfriend. But Al just laughed and said *not on company time* when Kent suggested it.

Humans had strange ideas about propriety.

But Kent was patient. In time, he hoped, he would understand them better.

"Hello, darling," the owner called to him from the doorway of the little gas station.

"Good morning, Geraldine," he said politely. "How is Juniper?"

"She's laying in her spot," Geraldine said, shrugging. "She'll be glad to see you, I think."

Kent jogged across the gravelly lot to follow Geraldine inside.

Kent was much larger than the average human - his body had been lab-designed to be big, strong and attractive. He had to duck slightly as he followed the small, older woman under the little bell that hung from the door to her store.

Kent gazed with satisfaction over the rows of cellophane-packaged snacks and the shining refrigerators full of cold drinks.

Juniper the cat sat on top of a box of car air fresheners near the large front window overlooking the gas pumps. The sun shone through the window at just the right angle to dapple her striped fur as she lounged.

"Hello, Juniper," Kent said softly.

Juniper flicked her tail as if in annoyance and he instantly felt the soothing green sensation of truthfulness the cat always brought. Even if she wasn't glad to see him, he was delighted to know her mind.

All of the aliens from Aerie possessed some form of gift

that made them a little more than human. No one was sure why - the scientists thought it had something to do with the process of migrating their once gaseous forms into human bodies.

Kent's gift allowed him to get a sense of the truthfulness of any given statement.

It had caused him some trouble when he first began to communicate with the citizens of Earth and learned a surprising fact:

Humans were confusingly deceitful in even the most innocuous situations.

That's why he respected the cat - she was always truthful.

How was he supposed to learn a new culture if everyone was always lying a little?

His brothers didn't share his dubious gift. They had gifts of their own, but at least they were able to traverse this new planet taking their host's words at face value.

"Can I help you with anything today, Geraldine?" he asked, turning back to the proprietor.

"Oh, no, child," Geraldine said. "I'm just fine."

But a red mist hung around her words as they left her mouth.

Lying.

Kent understood this falsehood, though. It was a simple lie of politeness because she didn't want to trouble him. Back on his home planet of Aerie, manners were very important, so he understood her reasoning, even if he didn't approve.

"I was bored today, so I came to see you," he told her carefully. "Are you sure you don't have anything at all that I can do?"

She looked up at him, smiling sunnily.

Kent loved Geraldine's beautiful face. Many lines and creases adorned her visage. Larger ones pointed from her nose to her wide grin, and dozens of smaller ones radiated out from her smiling eyes like sunlight through the trees.

When it was explained to Kent that the lines were from age, he was even more impressed. Each furrow demonstrated the tenacity of this tiny woman. She had survived many changes of the green and blue planet with both her merry smile and her store intact.

Geraldine's age had also given her wisdom, which she lavished on Kent with abandon.

"Never tell an older person you are bored and want to help," she advised him now. "You're liable to find yourself snowed under."

"I will remember, Geraldine," he assured her, though he wasn't one hundred percent sure what she meant by *snowed under*. He could puzzle out the words when he got back to his brothers.

She laughed and pointed him to a stack of crates in the corner.

"Soda man came today, and it will take me all afternoon to move those back to cold storage," she said. "I don't suppose you wanted a little exercise?"

"It will be my pleasure," he told her, striding through the rows of snacks to reach the crates of soda.

He eyed them up. Each crate held eight 2-liter bottles. There were four crates.

"One at a time, sugar," Geraldine called back to him. "Those are real heavy."

Without her admonition Kent might have forgotten and tried to carry two or three crates at once. He was exceptionally strong. But he did not wish to alarm his friend by demonstrating it.

He grabbed the first one from the stack and heard her opening the door to the back of the store.

It was good he had come today. Geraldine would have had to carry one soda at a time. It really would have taken her all afternoon to accomplish this task.

"Remember, always lift with your knees," she told him. "Not with your back."

He nodded at her advice and tried to picture how to lift a crate with his knees. How would he walk with it?

But it was too late now, he had already lifted this crate with his hands. It would have to do.

He followed her into the cold storage room and listened to her describe how her husband, Ray, used to throw out his back lifting up soda crates and other heavy objects the wrong way.

When they were finished moving everything, he hoped she would give him cold sweet tea and a snack cake, and then tell him stories about her adventures traveling on a cruise ship every other Christmas with Ray, before his death a few years ago.

And if Kent was lucky, Juniper would deign to descend from her box and leap effortlessly onto the counter or his shoulder to share his snack while they listened, making her delightful purring sound, which gave off a green glow of genuine happiness.

It was going to be a good day.

3

MARGOT

Margot staked out her quarry, hands trembling slightly from the incoming rush of adrenaline. The old bicycle leaned haphazardly against a trashcan.

Maybe it had been abandoned there on purpose. Or maybe someone had just left it for a minute and would be sad to find it gone when they returned.

Either way, after hiking through the woods all day and finally finding her way to the road, Margot was eager for a better mode of transportation back to town. The village was clearly farther away from A Slender Start than she had thought.

She made a mental note of the house number on the mailbox so she could return the bike later, or at least mail them a check when she got back to her real life.

Then she took a deep breath, darted out of the trees, grabbed the bike, hopped on and pedaled frantically back to the street.

She held her breath for a moment in anticipation, but

no one yelled out for her to stop. She took off down the hillside with the thrill of having pulled off a minor heist.

The simple joy of riding a bike on a pretty day was surprisingly exhilarating. Margot tilted her head back and enjoyed the feeling of the breeze lifting her hair and fluttering her grass skirt as she flew past the trees and cottages.

A few minutes later she hit a small dip in the road and landed hard with a jolt, nearly crashing back into the woods.

Margot dismounted right away and examined the bike.

The front tire was low, almost flat. It probably had a slow leak that had been sped up by the unexpected bump.

She looked back in the direction of the house where she had obtained the bike, but it was already well up the hill and out of sight.

She weighed her options for a moment, then opted to walk the bike down toward the village and hope to find a service station where she could fill and patch the tire when she arrived. It really couldn't be that much further. And it would be good to have the bike to take her wherever she was going after that.

Although she knew she should be frustrated, it was impossible not to enjoy the gorgeous day. The sun was shining, birds were singing overhead, and she couldn't shake the feeling that something wonderful was about to happen.

She passed a sprawling family farm with a welcoming, hand-painted sign:

Welcome to Martin's Bounty
Pick-Your-Own-Peaches Season is Here!

THE SMELL of the ripe fruit was absolutely intoxicating.

When she came around the next curve, her good mood got even better.

A small service station with a gravel lot awaited her under the shade of two beech trees. In the far corner was a pump with a placard that said *Free Air*.

She walked the bike across the lot toward the store. All she needed was something to patch her tire with and everything would be perfect. Hopefully someone was on duty today.

As if she had caused it with her thoughts, the door to the service station opened.

Margot froze in place, her mouth hanging open slightly.

A man was coming out of the store.

But not just any man - one that was so gorgeous it defied logic.

Tall, dark and handsome didn't begin to describe him. He was enormous, his muscles practically exploding out of his Hawaiian shirt. His dark hair hung long in front of his forehead, drawing her attention to his soulful brown eyes.

Whoa...

Margot gripped the handlebars of the bike so hard her fists went a little numb.

"Hello," the man called to her in a friendly way, his deep voice sending a little tingle down her spine.

"Hi," she squeaked back.

"Are you having trouble with your bicycle?" he asked, striding up to her confidently.

"Yes, I have a flat tire," she said, trying not to ogle him too obviously.

"That's too bad," he told her.

At first she wasn't sure what he had said that surprised her. Then she realized it wasn't *what* he'd said, but how he said it. There was something so sincere in his words. He was genuinely disappointed at her misfortune.

And he was closely examining the bicycle now, definitely not trying to look at her boobs.

While TV audiences might complain about her un-willow-y body, Margot's experience in real life was that men responded to her curves like kids in a candy shop.

But this angelic man simply ran his hands down the side of her bicycle in a gentle way that made her want to knock the bike over and hop into his arms herself.

"Your tire has lost its air," he noted calmly. "We'll need to patch it."

"That sounds good," Margot said.

Just then, a tiny older lady came out of the shop.

"Looks like you need a patch," she said, holding up a small repair kit. "Kent and I can help with that."

"Thank you," Margot told the lady.

Kent - that's a nice name.

The lady looked back and forth between Margot and Kent and smiled like she'd just remembered a particularly funny joke.

"Matter of fact, Kent can handle this himself," she declared, handing the patch over to the big man.

"Certainly," Kent proclaimed. "I can do that."

The lady gave a little wave and went back into the station.

"Let's find this leak," Kent said, heading toward the air pump with the bike.

"Wait," Margot said, feeling suddenly mortified. "I don't have my wallet with me. I can't pay you. Maybe I'd better walk. I can come back later for the bike."

"Don't worry," Kent said kindly. "I'll take care of it."

"Oh, no," Margot said. "I can't let you do that. I'm fine to walk. I like walking."

But Kent was already popping the tire off her bike.

"What did you drive the bike over?" he asked politely.

"I'm, um, I'm not sure," she said. "I went over a bump and it seemed to be flat when I landed."

She couldn't exactly tell him that it might have had the hole when she lifted it from someone else's trash can area.

"I found it," he exclaimed, holding up what looked like a tiny piece of a rusted nail.

She watched as his big hands worked on the tire, prepping the troubled spot and applying the little patch.

They were quiet for a moment.

"It's funny that we're both dressed for a luau," she told him, smiling at the thought of their matching outfits. If there had been someone like him at the party, she might not have been in such a hurry to leave.

He looked up into her eyes, startling her with the intensity of his expression.

"What do you mean?" he asked.

"Oh," she said, wondering if he was messing with her. "Just that you have the Hawaiian shirt and I have the grass skirt. We look like we should both be at a Hawaiian party."

He smiled at her and it was like the sun shining out from between the clouds.

"I see," he said. "I like your skirt. Do you have to water it?"

She laughed, knowing now that he was kidding.

"You're pretty funny," she told him.

"Thank you," he said politely.

He finished his work and straightened.

She noticed how big he was all over again. He towered over her in a way that she might have found intimidating if he weren't so obviously gentle.

She watched him fill the tire with air.

"Here you are," he said proudly, presenting her with the bicycle again.

"Thank you so much," she said. "I'm absolutely going to come back and pay you."

"It's not necessary to pay," he said, smiling down at her.

She felt that smile, a warm sensation washing over her. It made her bold.

"If you want to give me your number, I can be sure to come back when you're working," she said.

He blinked at her.

"I don't have a phone," he said sadly.

Wow. Margot had been rejected before, but never with so little effort to hide the fact that it was a rejection. Who didn't have a phone?

"Why don't you give me your phone number?" he suggested. "Then perhaps I can use my friend's phone to contact you."

Margot opened her mouth and closed it again.

Her phone was back at A Slender Start in the manager's safe.

Damn.

"I, um, don't have a phone right now either," she said.

They stood looking at each other a moment longer, until the sound of a car coming quickly down the road above broke the spell.

Margot pictured the manager of A Slender Start, a formidable woman who might be the type to stop at nothing to recapture a lost charge.

"I've gotta go," Margot said to Kent, hopping onto the bike and taking off without looking back.

She pedaled downhill as fast as she could, her hair and skirt flying out behind her.

When the sound of the car engine got closer she veered off into the trees and dismounted, her heart pounding in her ears.

A moment later a dark sedan passed. She couldn't see the driver, and had no idea what kind of car the manager drove, but she was glad she had avoided a potential catastrophe.

She paused a moment, half-tempted to go back to see the man at the gas station.

But the position of the sun told her that it was late afternoon. She didn't have extra time to drool over a hot guy. It would be much better to reach town before dark.

She walked the bike back to the street and mounted it again, heading downhill.

***

Thanks for reading this sample of **So You Think You Can Marry an Alien**!

Want to find out what happens when Margot ends up as an accidental contestant on a TV show where the grand prize is a marriage to the hunky alien of her dreams? Will Kent fall for her before he learns she's not who she claims to be? Will Margot be able to control her feelings for him long enough to keep her secret carry out her plan?

Grab your copy now to find out!
So You Think You Can Marry an Alien

Or check out all the books in the Stargazer Series right here:

https://www.tashablack.com/stargazer.html

TASHA BLACK STARTER LIBRARY

Packed with steamy shifters, mischievous magic, billionaire superheroes, and plenty of HEAT, the Tasha Black Starter Library is the perfect way to dive into Tasha's unique brand of Romance with Bite!
Get your FREE books now at tashablack.com!

ABOUT THE AUTHOR

Tasha Black lives in a big old Victorian in a tiny college town. She loves reading anything she can get her hands on, writing paranormal romance, and sipping pumpkin spice lattes.

Get all the latest info, and claim your FREE Tasha Black Starter Library at www.TashaBlack.com

Plus you'll get the chance for sneak peeks of upcoming titles and other cool stuff!

Keep in touch...
www.tashablack.com
authortashablack@gmail.com

facebook.com/romancewithbite
twitter.com/romancewithbite